WHISPERINGS
OF MAGIC

WHISPERINGS OF MAGIC

KARLEEN BRADFORD

HarperCollins*PublishersLtd*

www.harpercanada.com

HarperCollins books may be purchased for
educational, business, or sales promotional
use. For information please write:
Special Markets Department,
HarperCollins Canada,
55 Avenue Road, Suite 2900,
Toronto, Ontario, Canada M5R 3L2

First mass market edition

Canadian Cataloguing in Publication Data

Bradford, Karleen
Whisperings of magic

Sequel to the author's Dragonfire.
ISBN 0-00-648575-8 (trade pbk.). —
ISBN 0-00-648576-6 (mass market pbk.)

I. Title.

PS8553.R217W44 2001   jC813'.54
C00-932366-X
PZ7.B73Wh 2001

OPM 9 8 7 6 5 4 3 2 1

Printed and bound in the United States
Set in Stempel Garamond

for Jessica, Courtney and Brittney

"Always after a defeat and a respite,
the Shadow takes another shape
and grows again."

J.R.R. Tolkien, *The Lord of the Rings*

WHISPERINGS
OF MAGIC

CHAPTER 1

Dahl, ruler of Taun, sat secure and confident on his throne, surrounded by his council, his friends and his subjects. His reign had brought peace and prosperity to this world during the past three years, doomed before that for so long to the shadow of the Usurper. He looked up as a sudden commotion broke out.

A small orange cat that moved with the grace of a tiger and seemed to have a blaze about it stalked into the chamber. As it progressed, it created its own corridor of stillness through the multitude of people gathered there. Voices faltered, then grew silent.

Faces grew wary. The air was suddenly thick with magic.

The cat advanced to the foot of Dahl's throne and sat. It raised a paw, gave its whiskers and one ear a brisk lick, then shook itself and dissolved into a ball of light, so bright that all assembled there were forced to turn their eyes away.

When they could look back, a young woman with hair the color of flame stood in the animal's place.

"You have been summoned, Dahl," said Catryn, Seer of Taun.

CHAPTER 2

"It has been a long time, Catryn," Dahl said. He had spared not a moment in dismissing everyone who waited upon him in his council chamber, and now he and Catryn walked alone in the palace garden. His eyes were questioning, but he said nothing, only reached for her hand and smiled. He seemed willing to wait until she was ready to speak about that which had brought her here. The scar upon his cheek was so faint she could hardly make it out.

"It has, indeed, Dahl," she replied. "Three long years." She returned his smile, but behind the curtain of her wild and tangled hair, she looked at him closely. This was not the boy she remembered.

Of course, he looks older, she told herself. Still, it seemed as if it were more than just time that had changed Dahl. He paced beside her with confident strides, head thrown back, his light hair long and curling over his shoulders. His cloak billowed out behind him. Although almost of a height with him, Catryn had to make a conscious effort to match her steps to his.

He has become a king, she thought, and for a moment was almost shy. Then she caught herself. King of Taun he might be, but *she* was the Seer and as Seer of Taun it was her duty to help safeguard and protect this world. Dahl would need her and the magic she had learned during the past three years. He would need the powers she had striven so hard to develop.

For a moment, the reminder of why she had returned dimmed her pleasure at seeing Dahl again, but she pushed it out of her mind. We will come to that soon enough, she thought almost angrily. For now, for just a few precious moments, I will allow myself this indulgence.

"May we talk later, Dahl?" she asked, acknowledging his concern. "Could you first show me your city? Show me what you have wrought here? I have been away so long, there is much I would like to see and hear about."

"That I will do gladly, but tell me only, is aught amiss?"

Catryn's face clouded. "It would seem so." She shook her hair back out of her eyes. "It will take some time to tell. I would rather we speak of it later," she repeated. "Will you humor me?"

"Of course, Catryn. How could I not?" Dahl smiled, but his eyes remained troubled. He must know, Catryn thought, that she had a message of utmost importance for him. If he was anxious to hear it, however, he had his impatience well under control.

He has grown into his kingship so certainly, Catryn thought. He walks with such assurance. But then, she reminded herself, Dahl had known from birth that kingship was his right. He had been taught and groomed for his future role by the Protector since he was a babe. It was only to be expected that once he had conquered the Usurper who had taken his place as rightful king and enslaved his people, he would know well how to rule.

But she ... How different these past years had been for her. A lowly kitchen maid—she had never dreamed of the powers that would be hers. Had never had a chance to prepare herself for them ...

She set her lips and tilted her chin high. These doubts were not worthy of her. She had worked hard. Had learned well. She was as ready as Dahl to face what lay ahead of them now.

They walked through the gardens, then made their way through the streets of Daunus before they turned back toward the palace. As they neared it, the setting sun lengthened their shadows ahead of them.

Dahl was a well-beloved king, Catryn realized. He strolled amongst the townspeople comfortably and they greeted him with love and respect. Many curious glances were darted her way, but none dared speak to her. That was as it should be. A Seer should be held in awe.

She marveled at the color and brightness of the town. Where before, under the crushing rule of the Usurper, all had been cold and dead and empty, now all blossomed and luxuriated in the profusion of flowers, the bustle and noise of cheery, confident people. Dahl took pride in pointing out the changes. His voice brimmed with enthusiasm as he recounted all that he had accomplished in the past three years. But, even as she listened to him, the sun set and the air grew cold. She knew they could no longer postpone the inevitable.

"It is time," she said. "We must talk now."

Dahl nodded. "We will go to my chambers," he said. "We can speak there." He was suddenly tight-lipped; the enthusiasm drained from his face. For a moment—just a fleeting moment—he looked almost as he had when the Usurper's messenger had found him in Catryn's old world. But the moment passed. The glimpse of the boy she had grown up with disappeared. Dahl the King took command once more.

When they entered the palace, servants were lighting torches and candles. The hallways were filled with flickering ghosts of shadows as they made their way up a winding staircase to Dahl's own private

world, the world she and Dahl had lived in until he had been summoned home to Taun, her mother's magic had been feared. Feared to such an extent that she had been burned as a witch while Catryn was still a child. Catryn took a deep breath, waiting for the pain of that memory to subside before continuing. "The Elders taught me to cast my spirit into the farthest reaches of our world, Dahl. To see with my mind that which is occurring elsewhere. When I explored here to the south where you rule so splendidly, I could see nothing but peace and tranquillity. But when I started searching farther north, I encountered something strange."

She stopped as the curtain in the doorway was drawn back and a young man entered. He was dressed in a simple, coarse-woven tunic and leggings. A shock of untidy, almost black hair fell over his forehead. His skin was bronzed as if he spent much time outdoors, but he was obviously no servant.

Catryn looked at him in surprise. Who was so at ease with Dahl the king as to enter his chamber so casually and without permission?

"Bruhn!" Dahl exclaimed, his face lightening momentarily. "You are well come and just in time." He leaped to his feet, then turned to Catryn. "I want Bruhn to hear what you have to say. Bruhn is my most loyal and faithful friend here. His knowledge of the people has been invaluable to me. I could not have accomplished the half of what I have done without his help. I wish his judgment on this matter as well."

Catryn recognized the young man then. He had been Dahl's companion when they had both been enslaved by the Usurper. Catryn knew how much Bruhn had helped Dahl in that dark time and, it would seem, he had aided Dahl just as much in the time since then. She was slightly taken aback, however. She had not had time to get to know Bruhn before leaving to dwell with the Elders, and, truth to tell, she had almost forgotten about him.

"My lady," Bruhn stammered. He looked apprehensive. He had not been at court when she had arrived, but he had obviously been told about her extraordinary entrance.

Catryn suppressed a smile. She had wanted to impress the people of Daunus—it would seem she had.

"You are well come indeed, Bruhn," she said, gathering her wits about her and setting the smile free to encompass him. "But there is no need to address me so formally. My name is Catryn. Surely you have not forgotten?"

Bruhn bowed. He struggled to regain his composure. Dahl resumed his seat and motioned for Bruhn to sit beside him.

"Catryn has brought disturbing news," he said. "I would have you hear it with me and help me judge what it means."

Catryn's smile dimmed. She would have preferred to speak to Dahl alone. It was obviously not to be, however. She shrugged and resumed pacing. "When I tried to see into the north," she went on, "I could not. In the beginning I believed it to be a lack in my own powers and I strove to overcome it, but gradually I came to realize that it was something else. I consulted with the Elders and they, too, tried to see with me, but even with all of our combined powers we could not. We could sense chaos and terror, but also a numbness. A blankness. Almost an emptiness. It is frightening, Dahl."

"Could there not be some explanation?" Dahl asked quickly. "Is there really need for such fear?"

"There is more," Catryn replied. "A few days ago a man arrived in the country of the Sele. The Sele have remained close to me these past years, and when they heard what he had to say they sent word to me through Sele the Plump. That Sele is with me now. The man arrived sorely wounded and died before he could speak much more than a plea for help, but before he died he managed to tell them that there is a great evil befallen on the villages to the far north. He spoke of the enslavement of the people, of the devastation caused by a beast of great fearsomeness." She fell silent. She could see in both Dahl's and Bruhn's faces now a reflection of what she herself was feeling. A remembrance of the horror that they had all lived through under the Usurper.

"Surely not," Bruhn exclaimed. "Surely not again!" He had gone pale.

Catryn ignored the outburst. She spoke directly to Dahl. "The Elders have summoned you," she said.

"They and the Protector. I must take you to them and there we will consult as to what we should do."

Dahl returned her gaze. He did not answer, but his face was grim. As pale as Bruhn's, but the dragon scar that seared one cheek flamed blood red now. He rose to his feet and strode over to a chest that lay in the dark shadows at the back of the room. As Catryn watched, he lifted the lid and reached in. He took out a sword—long and heavy. The hilt glinted gold in the firelight. He looked at it thoughtfully, then back to Catryn.

"My father's sword," he said, his voice heavy. "Will I then have need of it again, Catryn?"

"I think so," Catryn answered. "And the Elders do as well. That is why they have sent me to bring you to them."

"And I?" Bruhn's voice startled them both. "I would go, too, Dahl. I have earned the right."

"Of course, you have," Dahl answered. "After all you have done for me and for our kingdom, it is no more than your due."

Catryn stared at Bruhn. His face was flushed now, his words loud and brave. Why then was she suddenly uneasy? She sent out a questing tendril from her mind to his. There was confusion there. And more. The beginnings of a deep, not even acknowledged, fear. She looked at Dahl with concern, but he was smiling broadly.

"I will feel better with you at my back, old friend," he said, then turned to speak to Catryn again. "I will ask Coraun to rule in my stead while I am gone," he said. "Bruhn knows him. He was one of my father's most trusted advisors and continues to be mine. I will consult with him tomorrow and begin making plans for our departure."

"It must be as soon as possible, Dahl," Catryn said.

"And it will be," Dahl hastened to assure her. "We will waste no time in making ready. But I must leave my affairs in order—it will take a day or two." He paused for a moment, then spoke again. "There is just one more thing . . ."

Catryn and Bruhn looked at him.

"I will go in the guise of a simple man. I would not have anyone we meet in those far lands know I am king."

Catryn nodded. She could see the wisdom of that. Bruhn, however, looked puzzled.

"Would it not be easier if the people we meet knew who you were?" he asked. "They would be much more willing to help."

"And more willing to betray us, perhaps," Catryn put in.

Bruhn scowled at that, but said no more.

"Now," Dahl continued. "You said the Sele was here with you, Catryn?"

"It is," she answered.

"I would dearly love to see Sele the Plump again," Dahl said. "It was a good friend and faithful guide to me when I first came to Daunus. Why did it not accompany you here to me?"

"The Sele have no liking for cities, Dahl, as you know, and even less for the buildings of men. It determined to settle into the stable with our horses for the night."

"Then I will go out to it," Dahl said. He laid the sword carefully back in the chest and closed it. "Come with me, Bruhn, my friend. You met this remarkable creature once before I believe, but only briefly. You will enjoy its company. Till the morrow, Catryn."

"Till the morrow, Dahl," Catryn responded. She watched as the two friends left, Dahl's arm resting lightly across Bruhn's shoulders.

Catryn twisted and turned until late that night, uncomfortable on the soft, pillow-strewn bed that had been provided for her. She had become used to a more simple pallet in the domain of the Elders.

She thrust all apprehensions about Bruhn from her. There was nothing to be done about that now— Dahl was obviously determined that he should accompany them. It was Dahl himself who occupied her mind.

Of course, I could not have expected him to be the same, she thought, brushing a sweat-soaked strand of hair out of her eyes. This room was much too warm. She tossed the coverlet aside. Light as it was, it seemed to be stifling her. He was still Dahl, though. Her best—her only—friend. She loved Dahl dearly and knew that he loved her as well. But things between them could not be now as they used to be. Before, she had been content to let Dahl lead. Reclaiming Taun had been his quest, not hers. She had insisted on taking part only out of her friendship with Dahl, not out of any feeling for this world that was so strange to her then. She had helped him, true. Together they had faced the Usurper who had taken Dahl's place and would have killed him. Without that help Dahl might well not have succeeded, but then it had been Dahl who had borne the brunt of the battle. Now Taun was as much her world as his. Now the battle that was to come was as much hers as Dahl's. And with the powers she had been given, it was she who must lead. She who would have the greater strength to face the evil that was threatening them yet again. Would Dahl realize this? Would he accept it?

She leaped out of the soft bed and stumbled over to the fire. Picking up a stick, she thrust and jabbed at the still-smoldering embers until the ashes smothered them and the fire went out. She threw herself back down onto the pillows. Then, in exasperation, she threw the pillows onto the floor as well.

She cast her mind out to the familiarity of the Elders, seeking their comfort, their reassurance. Their aura came to her almost like music, calming her, soothing her. She allowed herself to bathe in it and, finally, she slept.

CHAPTER 3

Catryn awoke, as was her custom, just as the first rays of the morning sun were fingering the sky. She lay for a moment, gathering her thoughts. Now that the time had come, there was a restlessness inside her that was urging her to go this very day—this very moment! She knew Dahl could not move so quickly. He had to leave things in order. Still, it was galling to have to wait.

She leaped off the bed. There was one thing she *could* do. She sped through the halls of Dahl's palace, casting uneasy glances around her as she went. Everywhere she looked was richness and luxury. It made her uncomfortable. This grandeur was too much for her. Dahl, however, seemed to have learned to live with it. The few guards she passed bowed unquestioningly. There was such an air of calm here—it seemed so secure. Her mind chilled at the thought of the rising again of the evil she and Dahl had battled and overcome three years ago. Who, now, was it using as its tool?

Even as she responded to the cautious greetings of the people who scurried back and forth in the grand rooms, Catryn continued to worry at the problem. Dahl had overcome the Usurper; there was no one left here who was anything but joyous at the thought of his defeat. But someone there must be, some-where, she thought as she made her way out of the building and into the cool morning air. And what was he doing to cause the chaos she and the Elders had sensed? The havoc the stranger had described?

She paused for a moment to drink in the freshness of the air. The sun, so like the sun of her old world, was just rising. Birds greeted it with song. The garden was heavy with the scent of dew-laden flowers. For a moment she allowed herself to bask in the peace, then she tossed her head and hurried on. She made her way across to the stable. She pulled open an ancient wooden door and was met with the warm, welcom-ing smell of horses. The air was full of soft, snuffling sounds and the occasional thump of a hoof. She looked around, searching for one particular horse. The horse with dragonfire in its eyes.

"Catryn, good morrow," a voice said. She looked toward the shadow of an unoccupied stall. A small figure, half her height, sauntered out, brushing straw from its body. It walked upright, as would a human, but was covered in a smooth, silvery gray pelt that reflected the pale shafts of light; its eyes were big and dark. In one hand it held what looked like some of the horses' grain. It raised the kernels to its lips and swallowed a large mouthful.

"Wonderful stuff, this," it said. "Almost as good as what we grow ourselves."

"Good morrow to you," Catryn replied, amused in spite of herself. Sele the Plump was one Sele who was hardly ever to be found without a bit of food. Its round shape attested to its hearty appetite. In this it was quite different from all the other Sele, who were sleek and slight.

"So Dahl is making ready for our journey?" the Sele asked. "It was good to see him again last night."

"He is," Catryn said. Impatience rose within her again. "I wish we could leave today, but he cannot."

"So he said," Sele the Plump replied. "He promised to get his affairs in order as soon as he could, though." It took another mouthful and munched thoughtfully. "I saw Bruhn last even," it said then. "It seems he is a most trusted friend of Dahl's."

"He is, indeed," Catryn replied. "It was he who helped Dahl survive when Dahl was taken prisoner by the Usurper and he who helped Dahl rebuild his kingdom."

"And he will accompany us on this journey?" the Sele asked.

Catryn looked at it quickly. Was there a hesitation in the Sele's voice? "Yes," she answered. "Dahl would have it so." She watched carefully to see the Sele's response. She knew Sele the Plump well. Trusted its instincts. If it also had doubts . . . But the Sele fore-stalled any further conversation on the matter.

"Good," it said. "We will have need of all the help we can get. Will you share some of my breakfast?" it asked, changing the subject decisively. It held out its hand.

"Gladly," Catryn replied. She was hungry now. Truth to tell, she was not overly fond of raw grain but during the time she had spent with the Sele while the horse recovered from its wounds she had become used to the food. That brought her mind back to the animal. She looked around.

"It is in a stall at the back," the Sele said.

She turned to Sele the Plump with a smile. "All this time I have known you, I did not know you could read minds," she said with a laugh.

A strange expression passed over the Sele's face, but it was gone as swiftly as it had appeared. "It takes no skill to know what you are looking for here, Catryn," Sele the Plump replied dryly. "Come, follow me. You will see that Dahl has cared well for the horse." It led the way into the obscurity at the far end of the stable. There, in the last stall of all, a huge dappled gray stallion stood as if waiting.

Catryn let out a cry and ran to it. She encircled its broad neck with her arms. The animal lowered its head so that Catryn could rest her cheek against its muzzle. Its eyes glowed with the dimness of banked fires as it whinnied in greeting. Catryn caressed the velvet softness of its muzzle. She had been the one to find this horse, and she had cared for the animal and nursed it back to health when it was wounded near to death. The finding of this horse had been the first indication that she had special powers. And, even more importantly, it had made the Protector, who had been so angered at her following Dahl into this world, begin to think that there was a place for her here after all.

"You will ride him on our journey?" the Sele asked.

"Oh, yes," Catryn answered. Then she hesitated. Dahl had also ridden this horse. Ridden it into that battle against the dragon of Taun where the horse had been so sorely wounded. And where Dahl had received the scar that would brand him for the rest of his life. Dahl had cared for the animal these past three years. Might he not now think of it as his own? She buried her face in the horse's mane and felt it shudder with pleasure at her touch. No. Of course not. It was unthinkable that anyone other than herself should be master of this horse.

Catryn spent the rest of the day in her own room. Dahl had his preparations to make; she would leave him to it. At dusk, as the sun was setting, she sank down onto the cushions beneath the narrow window. Closing her eyes, she raised her face, feeling the fading warmth on her cheeks and eyelids. She breathed deeply, then let her breath become shallow. The light behind her eyelids was rose-tinged. She looked deep into it, then deeper still. Gradually, the image of a glittering cavern began to etch itself upon the roseate background. Three long-robed figures sat at the far end of it. Catryn's breathing became ever lighter until it seemed she breathed not at all. She let herself flow into her mind, into that quietly shimmering vision. Dimly at first, and then with ever more clarity, voices spoke into the stillness. She listened until the sun sank beneath the horizon, taking the shadows with it, leaving soft darkness behind. Only then did Catryn open her eyes, but long moments passed before she moved. When she did it was to stretch out on her bed and fall immediately into a deep, dreamless sleep.

The next morning Catryn prepared to do as she had been bade. She ordered a maid to fetch a bowl of water. After the girl had left, she set the bowl down onto a low table, drew up a stool and stared into the liquid. The rays of the morning sun struck and reflected flatly off the surface. At first nothing, then, gradually, a thickening as of mist. The bowl ceased to be a bowl. The water ceased to be water. Catryn found herself swimming through the mist. She sent her thoughts ahead, probing, seeking the light beyond, but could not find it. The mist thickened until she felt it wrapping itself around her, holding her back. She concentrated, using every bit of power she possessed to see through it. Still nothing. Nothing but a dead, empty blankness. She knew not how long she remained there, throwing her will against whatever power it was that was blocking her sight. Then, just as she was about to give up, for one brief instant the mist dissipated. She saw trees, dark and hung with mosses. Beyond them a sense of walls, tall and foreboding. With the vision came a voice that seemed to echo and reverberate in her mind.

Come then, Catryn, it said. *I am waiting.*

Terror, swift and unreasonable, overwhelmed her. With one hand she dashed the bowl of water to the floor, then she collapsed, head buried in her arms on the table before her.

She was still there much later when there was a tap at her door.

"Catryn?" a voice called. "Will you come sup with us?"

It was Dahl. She raised her head, stood and took long, deep gulps of air. She saw by the light that came through the window that it was far into the after-noon—almost evening.

"Yes," she called back, willing her voice to sound

strong and steady. "But a moment, please. Then I will be with you."

She emerged to greet Dahl. Outwardly, she looked calm and unruffled. She had even managed to pull her hair back into a knot and tame it somewhat, although wiry tendrils were already escaping and ringing her face as if with fire.

"Will you sup with us, Catryn?" Dahl repeated.

"Are you ready to leave?" Catryn countered. "Have you finished your preparations?" The effort of controlling herself so that Dahl should not suspect how shaken she was sharpened her voice more than she had intended.

"Almost," Dahl replied. The sharpness had not escaped him. "I am as anxious as you to be away, Catryn, but there are a few matters yet to be discussed with Coraun. He will eat with us—we can do so then. And, further, I would like you to meet him. I would wish your opinion of him."

"If you have confidence in him, I am certain he will rule wisely while you are away," Catryn said. Her words were clipped. She still could not quite rely on the steadiness of her voice.

"I am glad you trust my judgment so well," Dahl answered.

Catryn looked at him quickly. Was there a wryness hidden in his words? Had he sensed her hesitation regarding Bruhn?

A wall of noise and smells greeted them as they entered the great hall. Long planks that served as tables ran the length of the room. Men and women sat at them, eating, drinking, talking to their neighbors and shouting to those farther away. Children ran about while dogs nosed indiscriminately amongst the rushes. Servants rushed back and forth, exchanging greetings and friendly insults with those seated at the tables.

"Who are all these people?" Catryn asked.

"They are the workers who till the fields, mainly, but any of the townspeople who wish to share our meals are welcome here at any time," Dahl answered. He smiled as he surveyed the comfortable pandemonium in front of them. "They are my friends."

Bruhn and Coraun sat alone at a table on a raised dais at the far end of the hall. They were talking earnestly, but their voices could not be heard above the general babble. Dahl led Catryn up to them, exchanging greetings with all on the way. Catryn smiled and nodded her head, but did not speak. Dahl took his place beside Coraun, then motioned Catryn to sit on his other side. Coraun rose swiftly to greet her, Bruhn a little less so. Was it her imagination or did a quick shadow cross Bruhn's face at the sight of her?

"Good morrow, madam," Coraun said.

"Good morrow to you," Catryn replied. She fixed her eyes on Bruhn in a silent command. Bruhn must know from the very beginning who was in control here.

Bruhn flushed. He sketched the briefest of bows. "Good morrow," he said quickly. The flush deepened.

Catryn acknowledged his greeting with a nod.

"I see you have learned the ways of power, Catryn," Dahl said. The tone of his voice was jesting, but now it was Catryn's turn to blush.

"As have you," she retorted quickly.

"True," Dahl answered. "You must bear with us, Bruhn, my friend." He reached for a flagon of wine and filled Bruhn's cup.

Bruhn essayed a smile in return, but kept his eyes averted from Catryn.

The table was laden with meats and cheeses. A pot of stew steamed in the middle of it all. Trenchers of hollowed out dark bread served as bowls, and more torn-off chunks of bread were available for dipping straight into the potage. Decanters brimmed with mead and wine. Catryn could neither eat nor drink any of it. All she could think of was the vision she had had that morning. She kept seeing those forbidding walls, hearing that doom-laden voice. He, whoever he was, knew she was coming. He was waiting!

Should she tell Dahl? Certainly she could not speak of it now, in front of Coraun and Bruhn. Perhaps later.

It was only with the greatest of effort that she kept

up her appearance of tranquillity. She spoke to Coraun about the preparations he was making for Dahl's absence. She conferred with Dahl about the arrangements they must make for provisioning their own journey. But she did not speak to Bruhn. Nor did he speak to her.

When they had finished, Dahl rose and stretched. "Then we will leave at dawn on the morrow," he said.

Now was the time to clarify the final matter.

"I will ride the horse with dragonfire in its eyes," Catryn said.

Dahl looked at her quickly. His eyebrows rose. There was a moment of silence.

Bruhn looked from one to the other, uncomprehending at first, then he realized what Catryn meant.

"Surely the King of Taun should ride that horse!" he burst out.

"Magic calls to magic," Catryn replied. "The Seer of Taun rides the horse with dragonfire within him."

"Of course," Dahl broke in quickly. "That is what I had intended all along. I will ride Magnus. That is my horse now."

Catryn could not tell if Dahl spoke the truth or not, but she did not dwell on it. It was enough that Dahl had given in to her on this. Besides, Magnus, a magnificent and mighty black stallion, had been the Usurper's own mount. It was fitting that Dahl should ride him.

"Bruhn has a favorite mount of his own," Dahl went on smoothly, as if there had been no hint of disagreement. "May we use the horse you brought with you, Catryn, for carrying supplies?"

"Certainly," Catryn agreed. "She's a calm little mare and very willing. More attached to Sele the Plump than to me. The Sele has its own mount, of course, and it can lead the mare."

"Then all is settled," Dahl said, but he made no move to end the meal. Instead, he looked down at the townsfolk who filled the great hall. His face settled into lines that made him look suddenly older. "Above all . . ." he began. His voice was so low that Catryn could hardly make out his words. It was as though he spoke to himself alone. "Above all," he repeated, "I must protect my people and my land."

"But are we to go unescorted?" Bruhn broke in. "Any one of those men and women—all of them!— would follow you willingly."

"I know that," Dahl answered. He nodded, still staring at the people ranged along the tables below him. Some of the children had fallen asleep on their parents' laps. The noise was beginning to abate. "I know well how great is their loyalty to me. But I will not lead them into danger. It is I whom the Elders have summoned and I who must do battle for them. This will not be a conflict to be won by armies."

"How will it be won then?" Bruhn persisted.

"That I do not know," Dahl replied. "But I expect we will find out." Finally, he rose to leave.

That was the moment when Catryn could have spoken to him, asked him to stay for a while. To talk with him about what had happened to her. But something held her back. Dahl did not understand her magic. Whereas before they had shared nearly everything, this was different. This they could not share. For now, she decided, it would be better to keep her own counsel.

Still, she felt a stab of loneliness as she followed him out of the hall.

The city slept as they rode out early the next morn. Dahl and Catryn led, Sele the Plump and Bruhn followed, with the Sele leading Catryn's mare. Once outside the city gates they fell silent. The sun rose; their shadows lengthened and kept pace with them. To the north, where they were headed, they could see cloudless blue skies. It looked calm and inviting, but nevertheless Catryn shuddered. She felt a prickling begin at the base of her neck and run down along her arms to her fingertips. The horse sensed it and danced a few nervous steps. Catryn calmed it with light strokes and quiet words, then settled her knees in behind its wings. Wings that were furled now and covered her legs with the softness of their feathers, but wings that could spread in an instant and carry them both skyward. She shook off the urge to do just that. To rise into the soft morning air and speed ahead. To see clearly what lay before them.

Not yet, she whispered to herself and to the horse. Not yet.

CHAPTER 4

Broad fields surrounded the city of Daunus. They stretched out flat and orderly until they ended at the thick forest that encircled the city. Although the hour was early, men and women were already working in them, tilling and weeding, tending small shoots of plants. Catryn was interested to see that Bruhn could address almost every person by name and that they responded with a polite respect.

"The people know you well," she said, falling back to ride beside him for a while.

"I have worked side by side with them during these

past years," Bruhn said. "They have taught me much about farming, and in return I have given them such assistance as I could. And I have been able to make Dahl aware of their needs," he added, a note of pride in his voice.

Catryn nodded, then spurred her horse on to rejoin Dahl. Bruhn had, indeed, made himself indispensable. She resisted the temptation to probe his mind again. She would not invade Dahl's privacy in that way; why should she then, with no good reason, invade Bruhn's? Still, a worm of worry gnawed at her. It was she whom Dahl would have to depend on now, not Bruhn, no matter how important he had become to Dahl. Would Bruhn resent that? Resent her for it? Behind her, she could hear him conversing with the Sele.

"I have heard much of your kind," Bruhn was saying as they entered the trees and began to make their way deeper into the forest, "and I would know more about you. Do you live so far away from here then?"

"Not so far," Sele the Plump replied. "We live on the other side of this forest through which we are riding. There the land opens up and there are vast fields of tall grasses. We live in them, but you will not see us unless we choose to allow you to."

"Why not?"

"The Sele keep to themselves. We give free passage to Dahl and his people, but do not show ourselves unless it is necessary. We have agreed that I should accompany you on this journey. The rest will help us if we need them, but only then. We are a peace-loving race and do not approve of violence."

Catryn listened to their talk but kept alert to the forest around them. There was something in the air that bothered her. She sniffed, almost as a wild animal might. There was one scent among the many others that did not belong there, but in her present form she could not make it out.

"Lead my horse, Dahl," she said quietly. "I must leave you for a while."

As if it understood her words, the horse stopped. Before Dahl could question her, Catryn slipped off its back. She took a few steps into the woods, then her figure seemed to shimmer slightly in the darkness of the trees. She disappeared. In her place, a lithe young wildcat padded off softly into the gloom.

She cast her head from side to side as she loped along, trying to separate the myriad of scents that assailed her nostrils now. Here a bird had rested briefly. Here a small woodland creature had crossed the trail. Suddenly she bristled. Here was the scent of a fleetfoot, one of the delicate animals that resembled the deer of her old world. The animal had been in flight, and Catryn's nostrils were filled with the smell of its fear. But flight from what? There were few predatory animals in Taun, and hunting for sport had been forbidden ever since Dahl had come to power. The Usurper's men had hunted before then. Hunted even the Sele. But that was finished now.

She froze and stared unblinkingly into the woods before her. One ear caught the slightest whisper of a sound. She whisked it in that direction. Nothing. She raised her muzzle to sample the air yet again. There was the scent that had bothered her. Alien, unidentifiable. Then, deep within the trees, one shadow, darker than the darkness surrounding it, moved. Catryn reacted with the instincts of the wildcat whose body she wore. One mighty leap landed her in the spot where the shadow had been, but it was no longer there. Vanished as if it had never existed. Frustrated, she padded in circles around and around the spot, but the figure was gone. Gone, too, was its smell.

"It just disappeared, Dahl," she said when she had returned and resumed her own form. Bruhn and the Sele had ridden on ahead and were still deep in conversation. They seemed not to have noticed her absence. Catryn kept her voice low. She did not want Bruhn to hear what she had to say.

"Perhaps there is a portal there?" Dahl asked. He frowned at the thought.

"Perhaps." But if there was it was well shielded. She could sense no trace of it.

There were portals in Taun. Doors that only those with the powers of magic could find. It had been through one of these portals that Dahl, Catryn and the Protector, who had cared for Dahl during all his young years, had come from her old world to this one. It was through such a portal that those who knew the secret could visit the cave of the Elders. But the thought that their enemy held a portal so deep inside their own land was frightening.

"I fear the evil that possessed the Usurper has been working hard these past years, Dahl," Catryn said. "You are not the only one who has been rebuilding."

"So it would seem," Dahl answered. He straightened in his saddle, his face grim. One hand tightened on his horse's reins; the other reached beneath his cloak to clutch the pommel of his sword. "You were right, Catryn. I have not been vigilant enough," he said. "But I am warned now." The cloak he wore was poor and threadbare, his tunic well-worn and patched, but, despite this poor man's attire, there was no disguising the nobility of his bearing or the iron strength of his determination.

Catryn felt her heart lift in spite of her misgivings. This was the Dahl who had faced and conquered the Usurper. Surely, together, Dahl and she could face this new threat. Surely, nothing could withstand the two of them. With Dahl's bravery and her power combined, how could they not triumph?

Then Dahl flinched. His hand dropped from the sword's hilt and, with a smothered cry, he raised it to his brow as if in sudden pain.

"What is it . . . ?" Catryn began, but in that instant the vision she had seen flooded back into her mind. The voice seemed to speak again. So real was the impression that she whipped her head around to find the source. No one was there. Nothing but dark emptiness and shadows. But Catryn knew with total certainty they were being watched. And in her mind she heard a mocking laugh.

The birds woke Catryn early the next morning. In the domain of the Elders she had lived amidst perfection, but there had been no birds. The gardens there bloomed perpetually, and the sun shone down from a clear sky, its blueness unmarred by so much as a wisp of a cloud. The land was green and verdant but curiously two-dimensional. It had taken a while for Catryn to realize what was missing: there were no shadows. It was a world of its own, silent and still, except in the deep recesses of the cave where the Elders dwelt. Only there was the rushing of water heard, the murmur of voices. In the three years that Catryn had lived with them she had never seen any being other than the Elders and the Protector. Food and every comfort they needed appeared as if by magic. And, of course, it *was* by magic. Theirs was a haven of magic. The core of this world. The center around which Taun revolved.

She crawled out of her shelter, stood and raised her face to the calling of the birds. Whiskers of wind brushed her cheeks and lifted tendrils of her hair. She drew in the deepest breath possible. Oh, how she had missed this! Then she shivered. Spring was coming to Taun but it was still cold in the pre-dawn darkness. She had forgotten about cold.

They had camped in a grove of trees shortly before sunset. Their evening meal had been pleasant. Bruhn, who seemed to be the best cook amongst them, had prepared a savory stew that had been more than welcome after the long day's journey. As they sat around their campfire, well-fed and warm, Catryn found that even she had begun to relax, in spite of her fears the day before. She could sense no presence near them other than the small animals native to Taun who preferred to hunt at night. Dahl and Bruhn had talked easily together and she found that she could join in. For the first time since she had arrived back at Daunus, Bruhn seemed easy in her presence. Perhaps she had been worrying unnecessarily about him, she thought. Seeing problems where none existed. She, Dahl and Bruhn each made themselves rudimentary shelters out of branches and moss and grouped them around the campfire, but Sele the Plump elected to sleep out in the open. It lay curled up as far away from the fire as possible. The Sele lived in grasslands that were dry during most seasons of the year; they were not fond of fires. They relied, instead, on their thick fur to keep them warm, and they would never dream of spoiling good grain by cooking it.

Catryn had slept well.

Now, in the early morning dampness, the banked campfire still gave off wisps of smoke. Catryn picked up a stick and stirred the ashes until they glowed. Then she began to feed the fire small twigs and encourage it back to life.

"Good morrow, Catryn." Dahl's greeting startled her. He bent to help her fan the tiny flames, then spread his cloak and threw himself down upon it beside the growing fire.

"Come, sit with me," he said. He held up his hand and drew Catryn down beside him. "I would talk more with you before the others waken. We had but a short time when you arrived, and there was much we did not speak of. I have missed you, Catryn," he added. His eyes shone clearly and luminously again. The darkness that lurked behind them, that tormented him so when it fought for control, slept now.

"And I you," Catryn answered. The feel of his shoulder next to hers was comforting.

"I had hoped you would return before now," Dahl went on.

"I could not," Catryn replied. She began to pleat the folds of her shift between her fingers, smooth them out, then pleat them again. "It was necessary to immerse myself completely. To forget all else but what I had gone to learn." She paused, remembering the last time she had stood in Dahl's court. After she and Dahl had conquered the Usurper, Dahl had refused the reward offered to him by the Elders of Taun—the gift of magic and immortality. But, as much to her own surprise as Dahl's, Catryn had demanded it instead. Her claim had been honored.

There was a silence. Was Dahl remembering, too?

"I understand," he said finally. "But tell me then, how does my Protector fare? He sent word to me regularly about your progress, but he did not come, either. I hoped he would. I have missed him, too."

Catryn hesitated a moment longer. She knew it would sadden Dahl to hear what she had to say now. The Protector had shielded Dahl from all harm while Dahl lived in Catryn's world. A shapeshifter, he had been the trusted companion who had prepared Dahl for his true destiny. No one else in that world, not even Catryn, had known the truth about the large brown dog that had guarded Dahl so faithfully.

"He could not come, Dahl," she answered finally. "He suffered more than you or I knew when the dragon you slew burned him in his hawk form. You know how long it took for him to recover—as long as it took you to face the Usurper and overcome him—but what neither of us realized then was that he did not recover fully. His strength was taken from him. Also . . ." her voice dropped and she lowered her eyes to her hands, fingers still busily pleating and smoothing, pleating and smoothing. "Also . . . he lost much of his power. He could teach me, but he can no longer shapeshift himself. No longer do battle with any enemy other than time."

"But he is immortal," Dahl said.

"Immortal, yes," Catryn answered slowly, "But he is not exempt from suffering. He is weak, Dahl. He cannot leave the cave of the Elders. To do so would be the end of him."

"He cannot die!"

"Perhaps not, but of what value would life be to him if he could not be conscious of it? If he became so weak that he fell into a sleep that would be in reality no more than a living death?" Catryn shuddered. The gift of immortality—was it truly a gift? Or could it, perhaps, be a curse? Dahl would never understand it. She could not truly understand it herself yet.

She spoke again. "You will see him when we reach the cave of the Elders."

"Good," Dahl answered.

"Being there will renew us," she said. "We will be able to plan our path forward. He and the Elders will give us strength for what lies ahead."

"As they did before," Dahl answered.

"Yes," Catryn replied.

There was another moment of silence between them, then Dahl spoke—so softly Catryn could hardly hear him.

"It seems like more than a lifetime ago that I first went through the portal to the cave of the Elders. It was the Protector who led me then. He was so strong. I thought he was invincible. I thought nothing could harm him. Now we venture forth again, without him . . ."

"But I am here in his stead," Catryn said. She straightened up and drew slightly away from him. "Do you not believe I can guide you as well as he?"

"Of course," Dahl answered quickly. But the scar on his cheek, a reminder of his battle with the dragon of Taun, flushed blood red. His eyes turned dark. For a moment the Usurper looked out at Catryn from deep within.

Instinctively, she drew back.

Dahl had conquered his foe not by defeating him in battle, but by accepting him. Accepting that his enemy was no less than a part of his own self, split off from him at birth by the powers that sought only evil and destruction. A necessary acceptance, if Dahl were to be whole, but an acceptance that would force him to face and fight against his own dark side for the rest of his life.

Catryn, too, knew well her own dark side. She had powers that the forces of evil would be eager to use the instant she gave them an opening. She dropped the folds of her shift and drew her cloak yet more closely around her. The fire was blazing brightly now, but there was a coldness within her that its warmth could not touch.

"What? Have you not even started breakfast yet? Sometimes you humans mystify me. Are you not hungry?"

Sele the Plump bustled up. It was munching with enthusiasm on a handful of grain. A loud yawn from the shelter behind him announced Bruhn's awakening as well. The first rays of the morning sun fell dappled and twisting through the trees. Bruhn's shadow preceded him as he unfolded himself and made his way toward the warmth of the fire.

They ate quickly, anxious to be on their way. Breakfast was a thick porridge that Bruhn stirred up in a pot over the fire. The Sele, of course, regarded it with suspicion and would have none of it.

This morning also, Catryn could sense nothing amiss in the forest. Nevertheless, she kept a wary eye on the trees surrounding them as they made their way through them. The path now rose steeply and they were forced to go single file. Sele the Plump led, for they were fast approaching its country. Toward evening the land became more level. Vast fields of tall grasses spread out before them. The Sele reined in its horse and turned back to face the others.

"Would you be so kind as to wait here?" it asked. "There is a stream over there that will provide you with fresh water, and a small clearing where you could make camp for the night. I would go on and report to my people if you don't mind."

"By all means," Dahl answered, just as Catryn was about to give the permission. She frowned slightly. She had come to think of Sele the Plump as her companion. But it had been Dahl's guide before, she reminded herself. It had been Dahl's friend before it had been hers. Dahl had as much right as she to command it.

Nevertheless, when Sele the Plump looked to Catryn for confirmation, she allowed herself a small smile of satisfaction, then nodded.

"We ask their permission to cross your land," she said.

"I'm certain it will be granted," the Sele replied. "We would offer you hospitality, as we did before, but I truly think you would be more comfortable here."

"Indeed, we will," Catryn answered. "We would not disturb you any more than necessary."

The Sele had taken Catryn and Dahl in after Dahl's battle with the dragon and the Protector's apparent death in his hawk form. Being much smaller than humans, however, they would have to erect new shelters for them as they had done before, and Catryn did not want to put them to this trouble.

"By the way," Sele the Plump added as it was turning to leave, "if you must make a fire, may I ask you to be extremely careful? We do not make fires here, not needing the warmth ourselves," here it patted its furry stomach approvingly, "but I know that you humans do like them for cooking and heat." In spite of itself there was a tinge of disapproval in its words. Apparently realizing this, it hastened to add, "We have no objections, of course, but if you would just ring it with stones, perhaps? Make it close to the water? Clear out an area around it free from grass?"

"We will," Dahl said.

"Absolutely," Catryn promised.

"Very well, then. I will leave my horse here and return tomorrow." It turned and made its way into the grasslands. Immediately, it was lost to sight, the only sign of its passage a waving of the tall grasses as it passed through them.

After the Sele had left, they dismounted and began to make their camp.

"Tell me about the Sele," Bruhn asked as he piled twigs and grasses up to make a fire, being very careful to ring it with stones as requested. "I would know more about them."

"As Sele the Plump told you, they keep to themselves," Dahl replied. "Not many people in Taun have seen a Sele. Except . . ." he stopped. He seemed to be having difficulty in continuing.

Catryn took over. "They are a unique race," she said. "They have no males, no females, no children. They consider themselves to be all one family and they are all identical. Except for Sele the Plump," she added, her mouth quirking. "That Sele is somewhat rounder than the rest. It is also one of the newest. Sele the Parent was the first and it is their leader. They do not really know where they came from, however, nor do I. The Elders have told them it is not time yet for them to know their origins or their destiny, but only that they have a purpose here in Taun. So they wait until that purpose becomes clear. They are friends to our kind and help us when they can. Normally, they do not die, but if one does the Elders call for another to go to them. There they cause that one to become two, and the dead Sele is replaced in the family. They consider it an honor to be so chosen."

"But how does a Sele die, then, if this is not usual?"

Dahl continued then, his voice suddenly harsh. "In the time of the Usurper he and his followers hunted the Sele for sport. That is why I allow no such blood sport in our kingdom now."

Bruhn stopped his work and stared at Dahl. "Did they think the Sele mere animals?" he asked.

"They knew well they were not," Dahl answered curtly. "They did not care."

Bruhn shook his head. "Much I knew of the Usurper's evil," he said, "and much I suffered because of it. My own parents died of grief when I was taken and enslaved to him, but I did not know about the hunting. It is a wonder the Sele trust us at all," he added.

"They knew my father, knew what this world was like before the evil encroached upon it," Dahl said. "They know we fight against that. They themselves will not fight, but they will help us in their own way."

That night Dahl and Catryn sat together by the fire long after Bruhn had retired to his shelter. Dahl was unusually silent. Finally, he spoke.

"We have changed, you and I, Catryn," he said.

"We have," she agreed.

"We are no longer the children we were," he said.

"No. We are not," Catryn answered. She tensed. She knew well what he would say next. Had been expecting this, but had not yet resolved what her response would be.

"When this is over," Dahl said, "I would that we could be together. I love you well, Catryn, you must know that."

"And I love you, Dahl," Catryn answered. "I have loved you for as long as I can remember. But now is not the time to speak of such things." She could feel herself flushing and was glad of the darkness that hid it. Her hands were trembling. She clasped them tightly together to hide them. To keep control. If Dahl realized how shaken she was . . .

"I do know that." Dahl stood up. "But when we return to Daunus . . ."

"When we return," Catryn agreed. To her relief, her voice was steady, even calm. But when Dahl bade her good night she could not answer. He bent to brush her cheek with his hand. For a moment it seemed as if he would kiss her, but he did not.

"Good night," he repeated instead, almost a whisper, then left her.

She sat alone by the fire for a long time after he had gone to his shelter. She knew beyond a doubt that Dahl lay sleepless in the darkness beyond the firelight. Was she making a mistake? Should she go to him? Could they not allow themselves the comfort they could each give to the other? She wanted to. She wanted to so much. She felt hollow with wanting his touch. With wanting the kiss he had not given her.

At that moment the feeling of being watched suddenly flooded over her again. But closer this time. Very close. She looked behind her, startled. Bruhn's shelter lay in amongst the trees, but in the instant she turned, the pale light of the two moons above gave her a glimpse of a face staring out at her. It was quickly withdrawn, but not quickly enough.

Anger rose within her, swift and cold. She whipped a tendril of thought out toward Bruhn with no pretense of subtleness. Let him know of what she was capable! But she was met with such a wall of anger that she drew back in shock, aghast at the depth of the resentment there.

CHAPTER 5

Sele the Plump returned early the next morning. Catryn had determined not to speak to Dahl about what had happened the night before. There was nothing, really, to tell. She could not prove to Dahl that Bruhn had been spying on them, and she was afraid Dahl would not believe the depth of Bruhn's resentment. He would think her exaggerating or worse—mistaken. For now, she would have to wait. But she, too, had been warned. In the future she would keep a close watch on Bruhn.

"Not ready yet?" Sele the Plump asked when it saw them eating.

"Do we have the Seles' permission to pass?" Catryn asked.

"Their permission, their blessing and their assurance of aid in any way we can. I'll just saddle up my horse and get organized. You won't be long, will you?"

"No," Dahl answered, leaping to his feet. "We are ready now. Are you are coming the whole way with us?"

"Of course. Did you not think I would?" the Sele answered.

"I was not certain. We most assuredly go to do battle, you know," Dahl replied.

"There are ways and ways of doing battle, my friend," the Sele replied calmly. It trotted off to where the horses grazed nearby.

When Catryn mounted later, the horse behaved strangely. It danced nervously; its wings fluttered and shook against her thighs. She calmed it as best she could, then dropped back to ride beside the Sele.

"We have not had a chance to speak since you returned," she said. "Was there any more news?"

"None," Sele the Plump replied, "but there was something . . ."

"What?"

"A general sense of unease. A feeling of worry. Not since Dahl regained command of his kingdom have I seen my people so perturbed. It is as if there was something in the air. Something hovering over us."

When they stopped for the night, Catryn waited to speak to Dahl alone.

"The Sele sense something wrong," she said.

"What?"

"They cannot say. It is just a feeling. As if something is threatening. I feel it, too. I am going to see what I can find out."

"Now? Tonight?"

"Yes. Darkness is a good cover."

"But how? A cat again?"

"A cat cannot go as far as I intend to. I must fly."

"A bird—you will go as a bird?" Dahl's face stilled in the dying firelight. Catryn knew he was remembering the moment when he saw the Protector, in his hawk form, consumed by the dragon's flames.

"No," she answered. "Birds were the Protector's other bodies. Those, and dogs." Her nose wrinkled slightly as she said the word "dogs." Catryn had not had much liking for the Protector when she had known him only as the dog that guarded Dahl, and she liked dogs even less now. "My forms are cats. Those are the bodies that fit me best. But tonight I will take the horse."

"Are you certain this is wise, Catryn?" Dahl asked. "My feeling is that we should stay together."

"That is not possible, Dahl," Catryn answered.

"I suppose not," he said, but he did not sound convinced.

"This is what I have been trained for," Catryn insisted. "You must trust me."

"I do trust you, of course I do," Dahl answered quickly. "But still, I worry for you . . ."

"There is no need. I know what I am doing, Dahl."

"I'm certain you do," Dahl agreed. "But . . ." He met her gaze. It was adamant. Giving up, he shook his head. "Very well," he said. "I will let you have your way in this. But take care, Catryn."

"I will," Catryn replied, but she bridled. It was not for Dahl to give her permission to do what she wished. Nevertheless, she was impatient to be off and would not argue the point with him now. "I will be back by morning," she said. "You need not fear for me." Her words were confident, even a trifle impatient. Clearly, Dahl still had no idea of the extent of her powers.

She turned then and strode over to where the horses were tied up. Her horse was not tethered—there was no need for that. Nor did she need saddle or bridle to ride it. She leaped upon its back and settled her knees under its wings.

"Tonight we fly," she whispered into its ear. The ear twitched, and the horse turned its head to look at her. Its eyes flickered and it whinnied softly. She felt it quiver beneath her. Without further guidance it stepped quietly away from the camp, away from the tree under which it had been sheltering. A few more steps and then the wings began to flutter. Catryn grasped its wiry gray mane. One tentative wingbeat, another, and then with a massive surge the wings spread wide and they were airborne. Catryn looked back and saw Dahl standing tall and straight, watching after them. His hair gleamed pale in the moonlight, his face even paler. How alone he suddenly seemed. For a moment she questioned the wisdom of leaving him. Was he right? Should they not stay together? But what use were her powers if she could not exercise them? And, no matter what her feelings for Dahl, her magic was something they could not share.

Then she and the horse were above the trees and he was lost to sight. As they rose higher and began to fly through the wisps of cloud that tried without success to hide the two moons of Taun, Catryn threw her head back and let the wind tear at her hair. For the first time in over three years she felt free! She had worked so hard, studied so hard. There had been no time for play. No time for herself. She knew this journey was not for pleasure, but in spite of herself she relaxed and let the moonlight course through her. The stars were calling. So tempting! Just to go higher and higher ... Forget this world ... Forget the terrors that were surely waiting for them ... Forget even Dahl!

"Come," sang the stars. "Come to us." A siren song, alluring, irresistible.

She closed her eyes and let the song wash over her, envelope her completely. Now the wind seemed to sing, too.

"Find me," was its song. "Seek me out. Fly to me."

Catryn lost herself in its music. The air around her grew frigid but she did not notice. Did not notice that her fingers were freezing into claws in the horse's mane. Did not even notice the slowing of her own heartbeat, the thickening of her blood . . .

The horse shook its head with a force that nearly tore Catryn's fingers loose from its mane. It neighed, a shrill, raucous shriek that tore through Catryn like a shock of lightning.

"No!" she cried. "Oh, no!" She forced her frozen hands to turn the animal. Down! She must get back down! Her chest burned as if with icy fire. She willed herself to take a deep breath, and then another, but it seemed an eternity before she could breathe again without pain searing through her. Gradually, as they descended, she felt a softer wind blowing through her hair, felt her senses pouring back into her.

How near she had come to being lost! How *could* she have been so careless? After all she had said to Dahl. Her cheeks flamed at the memory of her proud, overconfident words. She buried her face in the horse's mane and felt the warmth of it beneath her body. She breathed in its heavy, musty smell.

"My thanks, my friend," she gasped.

The horse looked back at her. The light in its eyes eclipsed the moonlight and the starlight both.

"North," Catryn whispered, forcing the words out from between chilled lips. "We go north."

The horse veered. Its wings beat strongly and steadily. They flew into the darkness.

The land over which they flew was night-black. Here and there a flickering light spoke of an isolated dwelling or two. Catryn pressed close to the warm body of the horse and kept her eyes fixed on the darkness below. She allowed herself to hear nothing but its wingbeats, feel nothing but its heartbeats. She was shocked at how easily she had allowed herself to be lured into danger. She grasped the horse's mane more tightly.

It will not happen again, she vowed grimly. Then, in the distance ahead of them, she saw a clustering of lights: a village. It was time she took matters back into her own hands.

"Alight," she whispered into the horse's ear, "at the village edge."

The animal circled, then landed soundlessly in a copse of wood just beyond the village green. "Furl your wings," Catryn commanded.

The mighty wings rustled as they settled into its

body. Catryn leaped off and threw her cloak over the horse's back to conceal them. "Wait here for me," she said softly. The horse tossed its head. She reached out to caress it and scratch its forehead. It made a low, snuffling noise and pushed its head into her hand. She rested her own head against its muzzle briefly, feeling the softness of it. Then she turned and walked toward the nearest light.

It was an inn. As she approached, the door opened and a few men strode out. They left the door ajar. Catryn shrank back into the shadows and waited until they had made their way down the path toward some houses. Then she drew into herself. Her body shimmered silver in the moonlight for one brief instant—and dissolved. A ragged orange-and-brown striped tabby cat stood in its place.

Catryn turned her head to survey this new self. A furball near her tail caught her attention, and she pulled at it with her sharp little teeth until it came loose. Spitting the fur out, she washed down the spot with her rough tongue until the pelt lay smooth again.

No need to look too shabby, she told herself. Then she became still and let her cat senses take over. Smells of cooking meat and firesmoke filled the air around her. She cringed as the overpowering scent of humans swept along in their wake. She was still not quite used to the odor her own kind gave off—a smell she never noticed unless she was in her cat form. She set herself to listening, each ear covering a different sector. Sounds, too, were much more distinct and much louder. Learning to separate them and not let them overwhelm her had taken months of training. Finally, whiskers twitching, she stepped delicately toward the open door and slipped in. There were but a few men inside and no one noticed.

Keeping a wary eye out for dogs, although she could not catch a whiff of one, she slunk along one wall. Snatches of conversation drifted over to her. Suddenly, one angry voice rose above the others.

"Never heard another thing from him. Promised he'd send for me, but he never did. So much for trusting a man—even your own brother."

"Went north, did he?" another voice asked.

The two speakers were sitting at a table near the fire. Catryn curled herself up on the hearth near them and began to purr. It was odd that she had never had to be taught that. She had been able to do it from the very first time she shifted, but she still didn't know how. It just happened.

"Old Tom did the same thing," the second speaker said, his voice equally indignant. "A friend of his sent a note to him saying there was work to be had cutting wood up there. He off and left and told me he'd send word back to me if it was true and if there was something for me, too. Never heard another thing from him. I figured he hadn't made out so well, that's all, and didn't want to admit it. Still, he could've let me know."

"Hardly see anybody from those parts down

around here nowadays, do you?" added the first man. "That's another odd thing. Used to be travelers coming by all the time, now—no one." He paused to light his pipe.

"You're right about that," the second agreed. Then both men lapsed into silence.

Catryn lay where she was for a time longer, but when they began to talk again it was about village affairs. She was almost hypnotized with her own purring by now, and the warmth of the fire was making her sleepy.

Time to move, she thought. She stretched, a long, sinuous cat stretch, then began to circulate around the room, but could hear nothing else of interest. Still, what she had heard had been significant. There was, indeed, something going on in the north. It could not be good. Strange it was, too, that there were so few men at the inn. And, now that she took one last look around and thought on it further, that they should all be so old. Where were the young men of this village?

She slunk out the door when it opened to admit another man, then trotted back to where she had left the horse. Safely out of sight, she allowed herself to return to her own body. This was something she must discuss with Dahl, but the night was early yet. There was time, still, to explore farther.

"We go on," she whispered to the horse as she settled herself onto its back and reached for its mane. "There is more to discover, of that I am certain."

They flew for what seemed a long time. At first, nothing seemed amiss. Catryn ordered the horse to circle low over small villages and scatterings of houses, but by now more of the folk below seemed to be abed. There were few lights burning. Then, just as she was beginning to think they must turn back, she felt a wave of cold strike her. The horse felt it, too, for it faltered. Before she had time to think, a wall of mist enveloped them. From flying in clear, sharp moonlight, they went instantly into a world of gray blankness. The horse began to labor. It was as if it were trying to fly through air that had suddenly become as thick as cold soup. Catryn could feel water streaming off its wings. She lost all sense of direction—could only tell where the earth lay by the fact that the horse was fast losing its battle to stay aloft and was descending rapidly.

"Turn back," she cried.

The horse banked in a wide circle, but they could not escape the mist. Catryn could feel its strands encircling her, reaching out and touching her like ghostly fingers, searching for her. The horse's mighty wings beat more and more slowly. They were sinking in spite of all its efforts. A glimpse of something reached out of the grayness below her and then was lost to sight as they strained on. Catryn caught her breath. It had been the topmost branch of a tree. They were so low! And there was a forest beneath them. If they tried to land, blind as they were, they would crash into it. Then, unmistakably, she felt the presence of something behind them. Something that was flying much more surely and quickly than they. A wave of hate and the stench of something worse than evil swept over her. The horse veered sharply and turned to meet the threat, eyes blazing forth fire. Catryn sent her mind out to meet it.

And was suddenly overwhelmed with such pain that she almost lost her grip on the horse's mane. She reeled, bracing herself against the blaze inside her head.

"No!" she cried to the horse. There was no alternative. "Alight! Quickly! Go down!"

As the animal obeyed, she fought to clear away the agony. She had to get back in control. She summoned up the powers she had been taught and cast her mind through the solid wall of mist. She had to see through it. She *would* see through it. Then, her mind broke free; it was hers again. The blaze of anguish was gone. In the same instant she could see as clearly as if the mist surrounding them were nothing but the lightest of veils. The outlines of trees stood out sharply, even though she knew the fog still bore heavily down upon them and all around them.

"This way," she cried to the horse.

It turned, obedient to her command.

"Now here!"

Again, it followed her directions blindly.

A clearing in the trees opened up before them. She guided the horse into a tight circle down into the center of it. They landed, then raced for shelter under the very trees that had posed such danger just moments before. No sooner had they reached safety than Catryn felt the fire reaching out for her again. This time she was ready. She threw up a shield around her mind.

From high above, a monstrous scream rent the air. The horse tossed its head; its eyes flamed. The scream tore through the mist once more, then there was silence. With the silence came a lightening of the air, a clearing of the mist.

Tentatively, Catryn sent her mind out to search. She found nothing. Whatever it had been, it was gone. Within moments the stars shone brightly again, and the clearing in which they sheltered became bathed in moonlight.

The first rays of dawn were stroking their way through the trees when they returned to the campsite. Catryn threw a blanket over the horse's steaming sides and rubbed him down, then went over to Dahl. He was sitting by the remnants of their fire, waiting for her. When he saw her, he leaped to his feet, his face alight with relief.

She cut short his greeting.

"The Elders and I saw truly, Dahl," she said. "There is something terrible going on in this land."

"Stir up the fire," Dahl replied. "I will waken Bruhn and the Sele and we will talk." When they were all sitting around the fire, Catryn recounted the night's happenings, but did not speak of the temptation that had nearly killed her. It was with a slight sense of guilt that she held this back, but then justified it by reasoning that it might cause Dahl to lose confidence in her. What good would it do for him to begin doubting her, especially since she had vowed nothing like that would happen again? No good at all, she assured herself.

After Catryn had finished speaking, they sat for a time in silence. Then Dahl spoke.

"The presence you felt pursuing you—know you what it might have been?"

"No," Catryn answered. "Only that it felt more malevolent than any force I have ever felt before. It was powerful, Dahl. If I had let it, it would have destroyed my mind."

"If it could destroy you," Bruhn said, "you with your powers, what could it do then to us?" His voice was brittle.

What answer could she make to that? None. Besides, she was in no mood to speak to Bruhn. She ignored him and directed her words instead to Dahl. "We must make haste to the cave of the Elders."

"Will they help us?" Bruhn challenged her. He would not be dismissed so easily. "Will they give us protection?"

"They will help us in their own way," Catryn answered, evading the question.

"What way . . . ?" His voice was even more brittle now, and rising.

"The Elders—they have their own wisdom, their own way of helping us, Bruhn," Dahl broke in, conciliatorily. "They gave us aid before. They will do so again."

Bruhn fell silent but his face was troubled. He did not look reassured by Dahl's words.

They took a hasty breakfast and made ready to leave. As they rode off, Sele the Plump signaled to Catryn to ride with it for a while. She fell back and allowed Bruhn to take her place beside Dahl.

"He is afraid," the Sele said, nodding his head in Bruhn's direction.

"So he is," Catryn answered.

"All this is strange to him, Catryn," the Sele went on. "He has had no experience of these things. Your account frightened him."

"What happened frightened *me*," Catryn said. It was not an admission that she would have made to anyone else, not even Dahl. It surprised her that she could make it to Sele the Plump. But it was not Bruhn's fear that worried her. It was how that fear might affect him. And affect the whole of their quest.

CHAPTER 6

Toward evening it began to rain. By the time Catryn finally signaled a halt, they were all wet through and miserable with cold.

"Is this place familiar to you, Dahl?" she asked.

Dahl looked around him. "It is," he replied, "but I would not have been able to find it by myself."

It was the spot where the Protector had first taken Catryn and Dahl into the cave of the Elders. The air here shimmered and had an opaque quality to it. Catryn raised her hands and began to make an opening in the space before her. She worked her way down. A dazzling light shone through, one spot of brilliance in the darkness that was beginning to surround them now. It beckoned to them.

"Lead the way, Dahl," she said. "You know it well. I will help the others."

Dahl nodded and strode through, leading Magnus. He vanished from sight instantly. The Sele stepped forward next, leading both his horse and the pack mare.

Catryn motioned to the Sele to go through, then turned to Bruhn. He, however, hung back.

"Now you, Bruhn," Catryn urged. She held out her hand to him.

Bruhn ignored her outstretched fingers. "I need not your help," he said.

Catryn raised an eyebrow. That attitude did not bode well. She shrugged. "Go on your own, then," she said, not bothering to keep the irritation out of her voice.

Bruhn stepped forward. He hesitated at the threshold, took a deep breath and pushed through. He had forgotten to lead his horse.

Catryn caught up the bridle. "Follow," she commanded her own horse, then led Bruhn's through.

The perfect garden welcomed her as if she had returned from a long journey. Warmth surrounded her immediately, but the silence here was complete. She basked for a moment in the intensity of the light that pervaded every nook and cranny and in the brilliance of the blossoms that spilled around her, but she could not stay to savor it. Dahl was already making his way toward the cave that lay in front of them, Sele the Plump close upon his heels. Bruhn stood staring around him in wonderment.

"It is beautiful," he whispered. "But there is no sound." Then he flushed and seemed to come to himself as she handed him his horse's bridle. He did not thank her.

It would seem my worries are not unreasonable, Catryn thought, watching Bruhn as he hastened to follow Dahl. He will cause problems. I should never have allowed him to come.

She followed him into the cave, her delight at returning to this haven marred. The air filled with soft noises as soon as they stepped inside. Catryn heard the trickling of the small stream that ran through the cave and supplied them with fresh, clear, cold water. Out of habit, she paused to dip her hand in it and sip. So pure! There was no water anywhere else that could compare.

The Elders were three. Two men and one woman. Catryn alone knew their names, but even she would never speak them aloud. The men were white-haired and their beards cascaded down over their chests. The woman was crowned with golden hair that glinted with silver. They seemed as ancient as the rock itself upon which they sat. To one side, the Protector stood. Dahl made an instinctive move toward him, then stopped. His face betrayed his dismay.

"Yes, Dahl," the Protector said, in answer to his

unspoken cry. "I am grown old. You see now why I could not come to you." He, who had stood so tall and strong, now looked even older than the Elders. More frail. He turned his eyes to Catryn. "You did well to bring him back to me, little cat," he said.

Catryn could not speak. Memories crowded in upon her. Memories of the quest the Protector had led Dahl and her on. Memories of the despair she and Dahl had felt at his apparent death. Then the aura of the Elders reached out to enfold her. She closed her eyes, the better to listen to the singing of it. It sang of welcome, and understanding and support.

Tauna, Mother of Taun, spoke first. "You bring news?" Her voice rang with the timbre of a silver bell.

For a moment Catryn was not sure whether the words had been spoken aloud or in her mind. She opened her eyes. The others had heard as well—the words had been meant for all to hear.

Catryn nodded. "I do, madam. And it is as we suspected. It is not good."

Tauna answered with a brief inclination of her head. "You will tell us what you have discovered," she said to Catryn and Dahl. "But while you do, your friends must rest and refresh themselves." She motioned toward an opening in the cave wall. "Go through there," she said to Bruhn and the Sele. "You will find all that you need for yourselves and the horses. We will call you later." The words were soft-spoken, but the ring of command within them was unmistakable.

Then Ygrauld, the older of the two men, stood. He looked hard at Sele the Plump. "I welcome you, friend Sele," he said. "Your race has done much for us in the past." He paused. "And you will do much for us in the future. You are of great importance to this world."

Sele the Plump bowed its head. For once it seemed speechless.

"And your comrade, Dahl," Ygrauld continued, looking now at Bruhn. "He is welcome, too. You are a brave man to accompany Dahl on this quest," he said to him.

Bruhn flushed again. He dropped his eyes.

"Perhaps braver than you know," Ygrauld added.

"But perhaps not," the other Elder, Ronauld, said softly. They were the first words he had spoken. The air seemed suddenly chilled.

Dahl looked up quickly but the ancient one said nothing more.

Sele the Plump broke the awkward silence. He picked up the horses' reins and headed toward the opening. "Will you lead Magnus as well as your own mount?" it asked Bruhn. "Catryn's horse needs no leading, of course." There was, perhaps, the hint of a reproach in its voice. It had noticed Bruhn's forgetfulness.

Bruhn scowled. "I would stay with Dahl," he said.

Dahl threw an arm around Bruhn's shoulder, but gathered both horses' reins and led him toward the opening.

"Not now," he said, voice placating, as he handed the reins to Bruhn. "For now Catryn and I have things to discuss that do not concern you. I will go to you later," he added, "and tell you what you need to know of what has transpired."

Not wise, Catryn thought, as she saw Bruhn's scowl deepen. Dahl does not know how much Bruhn resents me already. This can only worsen the situation. I must tell Dahl what happened the other night. Perhaps, after the Elder's words, he will heed me now.

But there was no opportunity to speak with Dahl alone that night. He and Catryn talked long into the dark hours with the Elders and with the Protector. Catryn spoke of what she had seen and what she had heard. She did not tell of how close she had come to entrapment, however, nor did she speak of the vision she had had in Dahl's palace. She was still reluctant to let Dahl know about either incident. The Elders listened and together they made what plans they could.

"We have tried in many ways to see into the north," Tauna told them, "but something is blocking us."

"You must journey there and discover what it is," Ygrauld said.

"And do battle again, if necessary," Dahl answered.

"Yes," Ygrauld agreed. "And it will be necessary, I am certain of it."

"Catryn has learned well," Tauna answered. "She will guide you, Dahl."

Dahl stood tall, his face as cold and set as the stone surrounding them. Only the dragon scar flared red on his cheek.

"I will not fail," he said.

Catryn thought of how nearly she had failed and her face burned. Was it truly because she did not want Dahl to doubt her that she had not told him, or was it shame? And was it shame also that had kept her from telling him about her vision? Shame at the terror it had awoken in her? Was she so afraid of Dahl thinking her weak? And if she were, was that not a weakness in itself? Questions she did not want to dwell on right now. She pushed them from her mind.

Dahl left, making his obeisances. Catryn would have followed but Tauna spoke, halting her.

"What is it that you have not told us?" she asked.

Catryn realized that she could hide nothing in this company. Slowly, reluctantly, she told of the magic of the stars. The calling that had nearly led to her death.

When she had finished, mortified at having exposed such a vulnerability, she could not suppress a cry. "So soon! So early on in our quest! How am I to lead Dahl if I am so weak?"

"You are not weak, Catryn," Tauna replied. "You are but learning still." Then she added, "There is more that you have not told us, is there not?"

"Yes, there is." Catryn said, resigned now to admitting all. She told them then of her vision. The looming walls, the voice that spoke to her. To her surprise, it was a relief to finally speak of it. The Elders' reaction was a surprise as well.

"It was a mistake, perhaps, for that power to reveal itself to you so openly, Catryn," Ygrauld said.

"A mistake?" Catryn echoed.

"Yes," Ronauld agreed. "He has given you warning. You can arm yourself now against him."

"Yes, you are right," Catryn said slowly. "But I worry about Bruhn. He is full of anger and fear. He resents my friendship with Dahl."

"The path Bruhn will take is not yet formed, Catryn. You must help him find the way, if you can," Ronauld said.

"And put your trust in those who go with you," Tauna added. "You have learned much, Catryn, but even though you have been given powers far beyond any that mere humans possess, you must learn to trust as well. You and Dahl must strive together if you are to save Taun."

The Protector rose stiffly from his seat. "Come with me now," he said. "We have work to do this night."

Catryn bowed her head to the Elders, then turned to follow his halting figure out of the cavern. Back, through familiar tunnels, into familiar caves. Her mind was full and confused. It was with relief that she set herself yet again to be his student.

In the morning they all assembled once more before the Elders. Catryn had not slept, but she felt renewed and refreshed after her time with the Protector.

"Approach, Dahl," Ygrauld commanded.

Dahl did as he was bade.

"Hold out to me your sword. Your father's blade."

Dahl unsheathed the glistening weapon and held it out in front of him, resting flat across both palms. Ygrauld rose and stepped down to meet him. He laid his hands upon the blade. As he did, time seemed to pause. For one moment there was a silence beyond silence. The sword began to glow.

"This sword and this sword alone will slay the evil you will face, Dahl, King of Taun." The words seemed to come out of the very air, deep and sonorous, filling the void. "Wield it well and with strength. But beware, it can be used for evil as much as for good."

All eyes were upon Dahl and the Elder. But at that moment, Catryn looked over at Bruhn. He, too, was staring, but his focus was on the sword itself, and the look on his face was one of hunger.

The parting was somber. The Sele looked as if it were well aware of what faced them, but that had not ruffled its usual air of calm determination. Bruhn, however, seemed to move as if he were in a trance. He kept his eyes lowered and would not meet Catryn's gaze. Catryn determined to speak to Dahl about him as soon as she had a chance.

She took Dahl aside as they were saddling up their mounts and loading on bags well stuffed with provisions.

"I am concerned about Bruhn," she began. "He is troubled and fearful. I think you should send him back to Daunus."

Dahl looked at her in surprise. "Bruhn is anxious," he said. "And he has every right to be fearful. This is a dangerous quest we embark on. But he is not a coward, Catryn. He endured much as a slave to the Usurper."

"I would not argue with that, Dahl," Catryn persisted, "but that is not the kind of bravery that will be required now."

"Bruhn is my friend, Catryn," Dahl replied. "As are you. You need not fear for him. And I would not for the world insult him so by sending him back."

Catryn took a deep breath. "There is more," she said, then told him about the night she had caught Bruhn watching them—and about the wave of anger and resentment she had read in his mind.

Dahl remained silent for a long while after she had finished speaking. He busied himself with tightening the girth on Magnus. He checked it over and over. More than what was necessary. Finally Magnus snorted and took a few irritated paces away from him.

Catryn wondered if Dahl were remembering the words of the Elder. There was doubt there, too, about Bruhn.

At last Dahl raised his eyes and gazed squarely at her.

"I cannot believe Bruhn would deliberately spy on us," he said. "And I cannot condemn him for what you say is in his mind."

Catryn felt her temper surge. Dahl saw it and reacted quickly.

"I do not doubt you, Catryn," he said. "I believe what you say to be true. But perhaps the fault lies with me. Perhaps I have not been aware enough of how Bruhn feels. It must be hard for him to take second place to you when for these past long years he has always been first in my regard."

"He is a danger to our endeavor," Catryn said, controlling her anger with difficulty.

"That I cannot believe," Dahl answered, shaking his head decisively. "This is my problem, Catryn. I will deal with it."

"It might be a problem for us all," Catryn argued. "I think he should go back."

"I will not ask that of him," Dahl repeated. "He is my friend. He has never proven himself anything other. I *must* believe in him, Catryn."

Catryn bit her lip. To argue further would only

open a rift between her and Dahl. That she would not do. Ronauld had said that the path Bruhn would take was not yet formed. Perhaps her fears were groundless. She would trust in Dahl's decision.

The Elder had also urged her to help Bruhn, a small voice in her mind reminded her, but she could not see how she could do that. What she *could* do was watch and be on her guard.

It was almost a shock to return to the real world of Taun. They emerged through the portal, leaving the sunlit, peaceful domain of the Elders, only to find that the rain they had left had built itself into a true storm.

"We cannot travel in this," Catryn declared. "We must take shelter." For a moment she was tempted to lead them back through the portal, then dismissed the thought. There was cause for haste—she could feel it in every bone of her body. They could not turn back.

They found a thick grove of trees whose branches protected them from the worst of the weather and huddled together under it. For the most part they were all silent, watching the rain stream down. It seemed as if each one of them had much to think about. By afternoon the rain lessened, then finally stopped. They shook out their wet cloaks, dried off the horses and prepared to resume the journey. By the time they were on their way again, the sun had come out fully and the forest was full of the scents of good wet earth and drying vegetation. The small animals that lived there also began to emerge from their shelters and scurry around. Catryn decided to ignore the persistent worry that insisted on gnawing at her and regard the clearing of the weather as a good omen.

"Our journey truly begins now," she announced to Dahl.

"It does," he agreed.

They came to a village before sunset.

"Shall we look for a tavern or make camp?" Dahl asked.

Catryn considered the possibilities.

"I think we should look for an inn or a tavern," she said. "We need to talk with the people and discover whether anything of note has been happening here." She did not think there would be since they were still fairly close to Daunus, but the discovery that their enemy might have a portal so near to them had unsettled her.

Dahl agreed. They made their way into the village. All seemed normal here. The road led through the center and was lined with small cottages. Flowers bloomed in front of stoops, vegetable plots could be seen on the sides of the dwellings and in behind. Smoke from fires issued forth from the chimneys of the houses. It looked as if most of the villagers were inside partaking of their evening meals. The few people still abroad returned their greetings pleasantly, without any apparent curiosity. They must have seemed just a group of weary travelers, searching for lodging. Certainly no one recognized Dahl as the king in his peasant clothes. At the far side of the village a tavern sign creaked in the wind outside a small inn. They rode their horses into the yard and were met by a stable boy.

"I'll stable your mounts for you," he called to them. "And rub them down for you. Nothing but the finest oats here. I'll take marvelous good care of them for you, I promise."

Catryn smiled. The boy was working hard in hopes of a few coins, obviously. She would make certain he received them.

"Thank you," she replied as she dismounted from her horse. A blanket covered his wings—she would not have the boy see them.

"I will care for this horse," Sele the Plump put in quickly as the boy came toward them. "We will be grateful to you for tending to the others."

The boy's eyes widened as he looked fully at the Sele.

"I am a Sele," Sele the Plump replied patiently. "We are a race that lives to the south of you."

"Yes, sir," the boy answered, stammering slightly. "Of course, sir."

"I will bed down in the stable with this horse, as well," Sele the Plump said.

At this the boy's eyes popped even more but he obviously dared not demur.

"Of course, sir. Of course. Right this way, sir. Follow me, sir."

"You may desist from calling me sir," Catryn heard the Sele saying as he prepared to follow the boy into the stable. He turned back briefly. "I give you good night, my friends. I will see you on the morn."

"Good night to you, too," Catryn called back, and was echoed by Dahl and Bruhn.

It was with relief that she walked into the welcoming warmth of the tavern. A fire burned brightly. They were shown to a table and within minutes served with food and mead. Catryn found her head nodding before she could finish the half of what had been placed before her. She had not realized how tired she was. But all seemed normal here. The room was crowded with people, full of noise and talk and smoke. None here seemed aware of any problems anywhere.

"There would seem to be naught wrong in this village," Dahl said, looking around as well.

"Perhaps it is all a mistake," Bruhn said. "Perhaps there *is* nothing wrong anywhere." He sounded wishful.

"Do you think I am so misguided then?" Catryn asked. "Do you think the Elders and I have brought you all this way by *mistake*?" She was weary beyond belief and careless with her words.

But it was Dahl who answered. "Of course, he does not, Catryn. You cannot fault him for hoping."

"I can fault him for doubting me," Catryn replied.

"I have powers you cannot even dream of, Bruhn," she snapped. "I have spent three long years learning to perfect them. Taun needs me and I must be obeyed. You *must* understand that. Understand it and accept it. I will not be questioned."

Bruhn leaped to his feet.

"Dahl is my master, not you!" He dashed the flagon of mead he had been drinking to the floor and stormed out the tavern door. Heads at the nearby tables turned. For a moment there was a lull, then the normal hubbub resumed.

Catryn looked after him. "I warned you, Dahl," she said. "He will bring ruin upon us all. Send him home."

"Bruhn should not have spoken so to you," Dahl replied. "I will make certain that he apologizes, but send him home I will not do." The words were firm, but his voice was not as sure as it had been.

CHAPTER 7

Catryn woke early, well before anyone else in the inn was astir. She splashed water on her face and slipped out to the stable. The stable boy was already there, grooming Magnus assiduously, but Sele the Plump was nowhere to be seen. It must have risen even earlier and was out about some business of its own, Catryn decided. She gave the boy a nod and a brief greeting, then set about grooming her own horse, taking care to keep his wings well hidden. The Sele came back just as she was finishing.

"Good morrow," it said. "Slept you well?"

"Very well," she answered, but it was not the truth.

Dahl joined them not long after. Bruhn was the last to appear. He was red-eyed and looked sleepless. Dahl gave him a meaningful glance. Bruhn flushed.

"I apologize, Catryn, for my rude words," he muttered, the words so low she could barely hear them.

She nodded. "I accept your apology," she said, her voice stiff and cold in its turn. Dahl looked from one to the other, obviously dissatisfied, but Catryn turned away. If Dahl refused to see the danger here, she could do no more.

They saddled their horses and made ready to leave. Catryn gave the boy coins enough to bring a cheek-splitting grin to his face. Catryn returned his smile. At least she had been able to brighten one person's day.

"The next village is about a day's ride away," Dahl said as they rode out of the cobbled stable yard, their horses' hooves loud in the stillness of the early morning quiet. "Or so I was told at the inn. We should be able to stay there tonight and perhaps learn a little more." He dug his heels into Magnus and urged the stallion into a faster walk. Behind them, Catryn could hear Bruhn and the Sele doing the same. In spite of the fact that she rode beside Dahl, Catryn felt very alone. How many more differences would arise between them?

They reached the next village that evening. It was as peaceful as the last. The following days passed uneventfully. They found nothing untoward in the villages through which they passed. Some nights they stayed at inns, other nights they camped under the stars. The weather held good; the people they met were friendly and welcoming. Some looked askance at the Sele, but were courteous enough to accept it once they had speech with it.

Despite the apparent calm and peacefulness all around her, however, the uneasiness within Catryn was growing with every step of her horse. At one of the inns, after the others had retired, she called for a bowl of water and tried to see again what lay ahead of them. She failed. She could see nothing but mist and emptiness. The vision she had had in Dahl's palace did not reappear, nor did she hear the voice again. She would have liked to think this a good sign, but something deep inside her mind knew it was not. She knew as well as if she had been told that the evil they were to face was waiting patiently, certain that they would deliver themselves up to it.

It did not help that Dahl and Bruhn seemed to have reestablished their former relationship. Catryn watched one night as they sat side by side, jesting about some small occurrence of the day.

It would seem as though we are on an outing for pleasure, she thought with some bitterness. Have they forgotten why we are here? But she could not help being envious of the easy comradeship that existed

KARLEEN BRADFORD

between them. Why could she and Dahl not have that? They had used to, when they were younger. Where had it gone? What had happened to it?

And then, as they made their way through a copse of trees to the edge of yet another village, Catryn suddenly stiffened.

"I know this place," she said to Dahl. "This is where I came that night."

"Are you certain?" Dahl asked.

"Yes. There is the tavern where I overheard those two men talking." She pointed to an inn on the path ahead of them.

"Well then," Dahl said, "this would be a suitable place to ask for lodgings tonight." He sounded resolute and forceful. Almost relieved to have finally reached the borders of his enemy's domain.

Catryn nodded. "It would," she agreed. But alarm was flooding through her, not relief. Every sense she possessed was on the alert.

Dahl turned to Bruhn and the Sele. "We will stop here tonight," he called back to them.

The Sele shook its head as usual. It would stay in the stable with the horses.

They left the animals in the Sele's care, then entered the tavern. As with the other taverns they had visited, a wave of warmth and smoke and smells of cooking hit them as soon as they were through the door. But something here was different from those other inns. Catryn stood still for a moment and tried to sense what it was.

"It is so quiet," she whispered to Dahl. "Hardly anyone is talking. And there are even fewer men tonight than when I was here before."

Dahl gave her a quick nod. The room was almost empty. The men sitting at the tables were either not speaking at all or talking in low, guarded tones, casting nervous glances around them all the while.

Even though the room was not overly busy, it was several moments before the innkeeper came over to them.

"What would you, my friends?" he asked. His words were brusque and he looked at them suspiciously.

"A bit of supper if you please," Dahl answered. "And perhaps a room or two for the night?"

The innkeeper hesitated.

"We will pay well," Dahl added, jingling a pouch of coins.

The innkeeper stared at the pouch, then greed won out over suspicion.

"Very well," he growled. "Follow me." He led the way over to a table in the corner.

"Your inn is remarkably quiet tonight," Dahl said in an easygoing, pleasant manner, as if making idle conversation. "Is aught amiss?"

The innkeeper looked at him sharply. "You're not from these parts, are you?" he asked.

"No," Dahl answered. "We have come from Daunus."

The man's face cleared. "From the south, then?" he asked.

"Yes," Dahl answered.

Catryn could sense the innkeeper's relief.

Dahl made as if to question him further, but the innkeeper forestalled him. "I will send the girl to see to your needs for something to eat," he said quickly. He hesitated again, then seemed to come to a decision. "Perhaps I can find room for you tonight," he added.

"For an innkeeper he is remarkably inhospitable," Bruhn remarked. Catryn noted that Bruhn had seated himself as far away from her as possible.

"He is worried about something," Dahl said.

"Everyone here is worried about something," Catryn said. "It is not like it was the other night at all. Something has happened to frighten these people, I think."

"It would seem the innkeeper, at least, does not want to talk about it, though," Dahl answered.

A young maid came over to them bearing mugs of ale and a huge platter of steaming meat. She looked as apprehensive as the rest.

"This is a gloomy place tonight," Catryn said, half-smiling at her as if to reassure the maid of her friendliness. "Is something wrong?"

The maid cast a quick, frightened glance at Catryn out of the corner of her eye.

"You do not know?" she asked, looking around to make certain no one was listening.

"Know what?" Catryn asked.

"There's talk ..." the maid began. "Talk about something dreadful happening in the towns to the north of us."

"Who is talking?" Catryn persisted. "What are they saying?"

The girl lowered her voice even more. "Several of our men have gone up there to seek work, but none have returned save one boy—and he has come back terrified and witless. He has barricaded himself in his mother's house and will speak to no one. She, poor lady, says he cannot speak."

"Who is this lady? Where does she live?" Dahl broke in, but at the loudness of his voice the maid gave a small squeak and looked at him in terror.

"I dare not say."

"Please," Catryn said gently. "Tell us. We mean to help." She threw a warning glance at Dahl.

"I know not what help you could possibly give us," the girl answered, looking again at Catryn, but keeping a wary eye on Dahl.

"Please," Catryn repeated.

"Her name is Mavahn and she lives in a house at the edge of the village. Just follow the path that leads from the well to the north. Do not tell her I told you!" The words came out in a rush.

"What is there to fear if I do?" Catryn asked.

The girl began to shake. She spilled a mug of ale, but did not seem to notice. "I know not what there is to fear," she said miserably, "but there is something."

"Rest easy," Catryn reassured her. "We will not tell."

The maid scurried off like a frightened mouse.

Slabs of thick dark bread were handed around. Catryn, Dahl and Bruhn were quick to pile their chunks of bread high with meat and begin to eat. Their hunger appeased, they began to talk again.

"The men you overheard talking the other night," Dahl asked Catryn, "are they here?"

Catryn looked around. "No," she answered. She saw a man at the next table eyeing them curiously. His companion sat with head bowed, a hood obscuring his face. For a moment Catryn's skin prickled. There was something about that form . . .

The innkeeper came back.

"I will show you a loft where you may make yourselves comfortable this night," he said, looking at Dahl and Bruhn. Then he turned to Catryn. "For you, I have a small room." The offers were made grudgingly.

Catryn saw the hooded man at the next table stiffen slightly. Almost, he turned his head toward them, then seemed to catch himself in time.

Why does he not want us to see his face? she wondered.

Much later that night, she woke. She lay for a moment, trying to puzzle out what had wakened her, but she could hear nothing. Nevertheless, she got up. The floor was cold to her bare feet. She crept over to the door of her room and opened it as quietly as she could. Her room gave onto the main area. She could see the embers of the fire glowing and sending out an occasional spark. A few snores told her that some of the inn's patrons slept there, stretched out on benches. Two men sat talking at the table where she and the others had eaten earlier. Catryn froze. One man wore a hood low over his face. Surely he was the same one who had shown such interest in them earlier on. The other . . . the other was Bruhn!

As she watched, Bruhn stood up. He cast a look around him that seemed almost furtive, then made his way over to the ladder in the corner of the room and climbed up to the loft above. Catryn watched him disappear into the darkness. She turned to look again at the other man, but he was gone. The table was empty. A cold draft suddenly swirled around her. She looked toward the door of the inn, just in time to see it close with a quiet thump.

Catryn curled back up on the pallet that was her bed, but she did not fall asleep again. What had Bruhn been doing there? It was possible he had not been able to sleep either and had gone down to sit by the fire for a while. It was possible that his encounter with the hooded man had just been by chance.

Even as she tried to convince herself, Catryn knew

she did not believe it. Somehow that man had arranged with Bruhn to come down after all were asleep and meet with him. He could have done it easily enough. Bruhn had stayed at the table for a while to finish his ale after she and Dahl had retired. The man could have spoken to him then.

But why would Bruhn meet him secretly?

CHAPTER 8

The next morning, as they were taking up their way again, Catryn moved to stand beside Bruhn.

"Who was that you were speaking with last night?" she asked, not bothering to give him a morning greeting.

"What do you mean?" He stared at her, eyes wide.

"I saw you talking with a man some time after we retired. Who was he?"

"No one. I do not know. Just a man . . ." Bruhn dropped his eyes, unable to meet hers. Then he blustered on, "Why were you spying on me?"

"I was not spying," Catryn began, but Bruhn whirled away from her.

She stared after him. His guilt was only too apparent. But Dahl would not see it, she feared. This was a problem she must solve without him. So when Dahl joined them she said only, "It would seem we should visit this Mavahn."

"Most assuredly," Dahl agreed. "Perhaps the lad will speak with us."

"What lad?" asked the Sele, yawning a little as he rummaged in his saddlebags for grain.

Catryn told him.

"He might speak with me," the Sele said.

Both Catryn and Dahl looked at it in surprise.

"With you?" Dahl asked. "I mean no offense, but why would he speak with you and not with any other man?"

"Precisely because I am not a man," the Sele answered. Its words were slightly muffled by the handful of grain it was chewing. "We Sele know something of what it is to be afraid of your kind."

"You are right, of course," Dahl said quickly. "Unfortunately, you speak the truth, my friend. Forgive me for questioning you."

"It is of no matter," the Sele replied. "We know you humans often take some time to see the obvious. It is not your fault."

Dahl looked taken aback for a moment, then managed a wry smile.

Catryn hid a smile of her own. I would wager no

one has talked to Dahl the king in that manner for a while, she thought. But aloud, all she said was, "Let us be off, then."

Mavahn's house was a poor cottage. Beyond it the forest loomed. There was a small patch of garden in front with a few scraggly vegetables growing in it, but they looked to be sadly in need of care. Dahl and Catryn dismounted just outside the tumbledown fence and motioned to the others to do the same, then they started up the path to the doorway.

Catryn caught a glimpse of a face at one cracked and dirty window. The door opened before they reached it.

"What do you want?" The woman standing in the doorway was thin. She stooped as if the strength to stand straight had deserted her completely. Her voice was flat and sounded as tired as she looked.

"Mavahn?" Dahl asked.

"I am," she replied.

"We have come to speak with your son, if we may," Dahl said.

"He speaks to no one," the woman replied. She made as if to shut the door in their faces.

"Please," Catryn broke in. "We wish to help if we

can. We want to find out what is happening in the north."

Mavahn's face closed. "You cannot help us. And the less said about the goings on north of here the better. Whatever it is, it has robbed my poor son of his wits."

At this, although her voice was shrill, Catryn saw the woman's eyes fill with tears. Catryn made a move toward her.

"But we might be able to do something. We have helped this land before ..." She stopped as she caught Dahl's warning glance.

"If I could speak with your son," the Sele said, stepping forward. "Perhaps he might be able to tell me what happened to him."

Mavahn looked at the Sele, her eyes widening now with astonishment.

"I am a Sele," Sele the Plump said with its usual dignity. It had become used to the people of Taun thinking it was some kind of pet. "We live in a country to the south of here," it explained yet again. "We are a peaceful race. We can be trusted completely."

Mavahn stared at it for one long moment. The Sele returned her stare placidly.

She must have seen something to reassure her, Catryn thought, because her manner slowly changed.

"I believe you," Mavahn said, but there was a wonderment in her voice, as if she had no idea why she should do so. She stepped aside. "Come in, then, all of you."

Catryn strained to see in the darkness of the room. The solitary window let in little light. No candle burned to lessen the gloom. She made out a table made of planks and a bench beside it. A basin and a pitcher sat on another bench under the window. Some few items were hanging from hooks on the back wall, but otherwise the room was bare.

"I did not used to be so rude," Mavahn said. "But things have changed. My son, Norl . . ." She stopped, then took a deep breath. "Would you like a cool drink? Water's all I can offer, but it's good and pure. Our well is a deep one and hasn't failed us yet, although everything else has, truth be told."

"Water would be most welcome," Catryn answered. Dahl and Bruhn both nodded as well.

"Not for me, thank you," the Sele said. "I would rather speak with your son—Norl is his name?—if I may."

Mavahn bit her lip. "He won't speak," she repeated. "Not even to me."

"I know," the Sele replied. "But if I might try . . . ?" Its voice was soft, but there was something in it that spoke of an implacable stubbornness.

Mavahn seemed to sense it. She sighed as she poured water from the pitcher and offered each a cup. "I don't know what good it will do," she said," but I don't suppose it can do harm. He went north," she said, looking up to include Dahl and Catryn, "to seek work. There is little to be had around these parts, and we had heard things were better to the north. That was before the stories started drifting back."

"Stories?" Catryn asked, but Dahl interrupted her. "Why is there no work? What is wrong here?"

"It is because of the bad times."

"The bad times?"

"Yes. You know. You must know. When the evil king they now call the Usurper ruled. He sent his soldiers to capture our young men to work for him and none were left to follow the trades here. My husband was taken and, like most of the others, did not return when our good King Dahl conquered the Usurper. We heard most of that evil man's slaves died. I can only suppose my husband did as well." Her voice broke.

Catryn glanced sideways at Dahl, but he was staring at the woman. His face betrayed nothing, although the dragon scar flared briefly. He raised his hand instinctively to hide it, but Mavahn seemed not to notice. She made an effort to control herself, then continued. "The men who were left were old and there were no young ones to pass their knowledge on to. We have no blacksmith now, so our horses go unshod and cannot work. We have no miller, so our mills grind no grain. We have so few young men that our young women leave the village to seek husbands elsewhere. My son, Norl, was but a child then, almost a babe. He escaped being taken into slavery, but now there is no one left to teach him a craft. He was desperate and believed the rumors we heard that there was work to be had in the north. Much too young, he was, but he ran off without telling me, determined to go there and find a way to earn some coins. But the rumors were lies—all lies! Whatever happened to him there, it has all but destroyed him. He has come back broken, but he cannot tell of it. Not even to me."

Mavahn turned back to the Sele. "I know not why it should be any different with you, but there is something about you that inspires confidence. I believe that you can be trusted." Her eyes filled again and spilled over. Tears made their way down her cheeks. "If there is anything you can do to help him . . ."

Catryn caught a sudden movement out of the corner of her eye. Beside her, Bruhn was staring at Mavahn, his face twisted in pain. Suddenly, he turned on his heel and stumbled back out the door. The fate of the young men of Mavahn's village must have been all too real for him, Catryn realized. He had lived most of his younger years in slavery to the Usurper; he knew all too well what it had been like. For a moment she was tempted to follow him. Perhaps now he would speak to her. This might be her opportunity to reach him. But there were questions she had to ask. The mystery of the old men in the tavern was solved, but she had to learn more about the danger that threatened them all. She let Bruhn go and turned back to Mavahn.

"What *are* the stories are coming out of the north now?" she asked.

Mavahn's face closed again. "Impossible tales. Tales of monsters and sudden darkness and the dying of the sun. I will not listen to them. They are lies, just as the promises that were made before were lies. They must be. Such things do not happen."

"But something did happen to Norl," the Sele persisted. "Will you take me to him?"

"Very well. Try if you must." Mavahn's voice had gone dead again. Whatever faint hope there had been in it before had vanished.

"That I will," the Sele said.

Mavahn led the way into the other room, with Sele the Plump following closely behind.

Dahl looked around. "Where is Bruhn?" he asked.

"He left," Catryn replied. "He was upset at hearing what Mavahn had to say."

"As am I," Dahl replied. "It seems you and the Elders saw truly, Catryn."

At that moment, Mavahn reentered the room.

"That Sele—it is a remarkable animal," she said.

"It is not an animal," Catryn said.

"Forgive me, I do not quite know what it is," Mavahn said. "But it was right. Norl does seem to trust him. He did not speak while I was there, but for the first time since his return I saw some of the fear leave his eyes. That boy was a gift that came to me in answer to my prayers—I pray now your Sele will be able to help him."

Catryn sat on the bench beside Dahl, staring at the door to the room where the Sele spoke with Mavahn's son. They had been sequestered in there for a very long time now. What was going on? Mavahn seemed possessed of an urgent nervousness that would not let her remain still. She paced the small confines of this room without ceasing. It grated on Catryn's own nerves to such an extent that it took all of her willpower not to shout at the woman— command her to stop—but she held her tongue. She could only imagine the pain the woman must be suffering. To lose her husband, and now her son. She was young, too, not as old as Catryn had originally believed. Dahl seemed sunk in thought. Bruhn had not reappeared.

Both Catryn and Dahl jumped when the door to the other room finally opened. Mavahn stopped in mid-stride. Sele the Plump walked out, followed by a boy. Probably not more than twelve years of age, Catryn judged, and small even for that. His dark hair fell over downcast eyes. He wore a short, woolen tunic, much patched but clean. His hands fidgeted with the folds and wound themselves around the rope that encircled his waist.

"I have spoken with Norl," Sele the Plump

announced. "He has, indeed, seen horrific sights and endured much."

"He spoke?" Mavahn's voice was a whisper as she stared into her son's face.

"He spoke," the Sele replied. He turned to the boy. "Tell them, boy," it said gently. "Your mother needs to hear your words."

Norl looked back at his mother. "I'm sorry, Mother," he said. "I've worried you, but I didn't mean to." The words wobbled and shook.

Mavahn let out a cry and swooped down upon him, enveloping him in her arms. "Norl!" she cried. "Thanks be! You've come back to me!"

At that the boy collapsed onto her shoulder and he, too, wept.

"What did you see in the north?" Dahl asked. "What happened there?"

Mavahn grasped her son tightly and glared at Dahl over his shoulders. "Question him not!" she cried. "I will not have him troubled again. He must forget!"

But Norl straightened and turned to face Dahl. He dashed the tears from his eyes with one hand. His face was pale but set. "It's all right, Mother," he said. "I can speak of what I saw now." He flashed a look at Sele the Plump and drew a deep breath, as if drawing breath from the Sele itself, then looked back at Dahl.

"I saw a monster, horrible beyond all description. It flew over me and descended upon the village I was walking toward. The marketplace was crowded with people. They screamed and began running every which way, but it flew low over them, covering them with its shadow." Norl stopped. Mavahn drew him closer.

"Enough, child. That's enough."

"No, Mother, I must finish." He went on, shuddering. "A darkness rose up from the ground—all shredded and in pieces. The monster . . . the monster seemed somehow to gather it all into one huge cloud and then sped off through the skies, trailing the cloud behind it."

"This monster," Dahl said, his voice tight with strain, "did it spew forth fire?"

"No," Norl answered, "but its eyes glowed as if there were flames burning behind them."

"Dragonfire," Dahl breathed. "But how can it be? I slew the dragon myself!"

"You slew one dragon, Dahl. This must be another," Catryn said. "This must be the beast that pursued me the night the horse and I flew up here."

"A dragon?" The voice from the doorway startled them all. Bruhn stood there. "We go to do battle with a *dragon*?"

"I have done battle with a dragon before. If needs be I will do battle with a dragon again," Dahl answered.

"There is more amiss here than just a dragon," Catryn said thoughtfully.

"*Just* a dragon?" Bruhn echoed. "I should think a dragon would be danger enough!"

Catryn paid him no heed. She directed her next

question to Norl, as gently as she could.

"The people, Norl . . . What did the people do after the beast flew away?"

For a moment Norl looked confused. "I turned and ran," he said. "I was too frightened to look back, but . . ."

"But?" Catryn encouraged him.

"But before I fled I saw the people standing there. Just standing where they had been when the monster attacked. And they were not screaming anymore . . ." He stared at Catryn, confusion mounting in his face as he remembered. "They were not making any noise at all. They just—*stood* there."

"We must go to that village," Dahl said. "As quickly as we can. We *must* find out what is happening."

As they made their farewells, Catryn's mind was churning. Norl's description of what had happened—the chaos, then the strange silence, the numbness of the people—that description matched so exactly what she had felt when she had tried seeing into the north. She turned to take a last look back at the boy and his mother, then suddenly she stiffened. Surely that was not the figure of a man she saw duck into the trees behind the house? A hooded man?

CHAPTER 9

They traveled all that day without reaching another village. At sundown Catryn and Dahl determined to make camp in a welcoming grove of trees. The weather was warm. Small insects tormented them while they settled themselves, but as soon as the fire was smoking the bugs desisted. Bruhn soon had a good stew boiling over the flames; the Sele ate naught but his grain. Catryn and Dahl discussed what they had learned from the boy, Norl, while they ate, but Bruhn remained silent. As soon as they had finished eating, he spread his cloak out under a tree and settled himself for sleep. Catryn waited by the fire until she was certain he slept. She had decided that she must speak to Dahl again about Bruhn, whether he wished to hear it or not.

Dahl had moved away from the campfire. He was sitting, staring at the two moons that were rising above the trees, one just slightly above the other. Their combined light etched the copse in which they camped into sharp black-and-white shadows, in some cases, shadows that were twins of each other.

"Dahl?"

He looked up. Catryn dropped down to the leaf-strewn ground beside him. Somewhere close, a small animal scurried into hiding.

"I would talk further with you about Bruhn."

"What now, Catryn?" Dahl asked wearily.

"After we went to our beds in the tavern last night I felt uneasy," she began. "Something was bothering me. I knew not what. I opened the door of my room and looked out into the tavern. Bruhn was there. He had returned after he thought that we all slept, and he was deep in conversation with a man."

"Perhaps he could not sleep, either," Dahl said, but the frown returned to furrow his brow.

"Wait. Hear me out," Catryn said. "I had noticed this man earlier, while we supped. He sat at the table next to us and seemed to be trying to hear all that we said, but he kept his face covered with his hood. As if he did not want us to see him. And there was something about him. Something familiar. Something that made my skin prickle in warning."

"What are you saying now, Catryn? That Bruhn is not to be trusted? That he is plotting against us?"

"No," Catryn exclaimed, then glanced around to ensure the others had not heard her. She lowered her voice. "No," she repeated. "I am not saying that, but Bruhn looked so furtive. And when I questioned him about it he lied to me."

"Perhaps he was angered again by your suspicions. You have been hard on him, Catryn," Dahl said. Nevertheless, he leaped to his feet and began to pace. His hands clenched.

"That is not all," Catryn answered, forcing herself to speak calmly. "I saw that man again when we left Mavahn's cottage. He is following us."

"How do you know it was the same man?" Dahl demanded. "Did you see his face at all?"

"No," Catryn answered. "He was hooded every time I saw him. But I am certain it was the same man. And I know he means danger for us."

Dahl ceased his pacing and stood. He, too, seemed to be struggling to control himself. "Forgive me, Catryn," he said. "I recognize your abilities and I welcome your help, but I fear you are seeing problems where there are none. Bruhn may be afraid—I can accept that—but I cannot believe he is plotting against us."

"I did not say that . . ." Catryn began. She felt a sinking of her heart. She was just making matters worse.

"But that *is* what you are saying," Dahl countered.

Catryn fell silent. He was right.

"I will not lose faith with Bruhn because of suspicions, Catryn. If you have proof, come to me with it. If not, I wish to hear no more of this."

Catryn's face closed. So be it. Let whatever Bruhn might do be on Dahl's head. She retreated to her own shelter and curled herself up, wrapped in anger. She felt the aura of the Elders reaching out to her, but she did not open herself to it. Her mind was too full, too troubled. She could not let them comfort her.

The moons reached their apex and started their journey back down to the far horizon. Still, Catryn lay sleepless. Finally, she gave up even trying to find rest. She crept out of her shelter and walked into the trees that surrounded them. The soft, hidden noises of the night began to soothe her. Then another noise, not loud but out of place in this peace, stopped her. Quickly, she slipped off the path and concealed herself behind a tree. Coming up the path, in the direction from which they had traveled, came a figure. Darkness swirled around him as his cape billowed with each careful step. She knew him! Catryn did not pause for thought. She gathered into herself and melted into the darkness. Immediately, she became one with the night and its secrets opened to her. Black fur shimmered; unblinking, ebonite eyes glittered. She padded slowly and silently after him, the hard-packed forest floor reassuringly solid beneath her paws.

The man made his way straight toward their camp. At the edge of the clearing he paused to survey the small cluster of shelters. Catryn slipped through the trees behind him. As she drew near to him, her ears flattened against her head.

A mist of evil swam through the darkness to Catryn. Instinctively she drew back her lips, baring teeth that gleamed in the failing light of the two moons. A low growl began deep in her throat. A mistake. The man stiffened. He turned, but his face was still hidden in the shadow of his hood.

They faced each other as if waiting to do battle. Catryn tensed her muscles to spring. She felt her claws clench into the ground beneath her feet. At that moment, as if he had been called, Bruhn stepped out of his shelter. The man looked over his shoulder at Bruhn, then back at Catryn. He drew his cloak around him and vanished just as she sprang.

She landed in empty space. Bruhn stared at her from across the dwindling fire in astonishment. Catryn whirled and disappeared back into the trees. Now Dahl *must* listen to her!

"Catryn tells an extraordinary tale, Bruhn," Dahl said the next morning as they were readying to leave.

Bruhn dropped the water jug he was holding. He recovered himself quickly, but his hands trembled as he bent to retrieve the vessel before too much water spilled out.

"She tells of a man who came to our campsite in the dead of night last night. Who stood gazing at us as if calling to someone. And you coming out to meet him. Is this true, my friend? What is the explanation?"

"So now you doubt me, too?" Bruhn exploded. "You call me friend, but you question me because of *her* suspicions?"

"I am but asking, Bruhn. What can you tell me?"

"I saw no man," Bruhn blustered. "I came out in the night to relieve myself. If there was a man watching, I did not see him."

"Is this true, my friend?"

"Do you accuse me of lying in the same breath that you call me friend?" Bruhn asked through clenched teeth.

"No, of course not," Dahl responded quickly, but his voice lacked conviction.

Bruhn turned on his heel and left. Dahl would have followed, but Catryn forestalled him.

"There was a man there, Dahl," Catryn insisted, "and he was no ordinary man." Finally, she told him of the vision she had had in his palace.

"Why did you not tell me this before?" Dahl demanded. "I should have known of it."

"You are right. I should have spoken of this earlier," Catryn answered. "I did not want you to know how frightened I was by it. I was afraid ... afraid you would lose confidence in me if you knew how vulnerable I was."

"I would never have done so, Catryn," Dahl exclaimed. "Fear is not to be ashamed of. I learned that well when I faced the Usurper. No one could have been more afraid than I was then. But the Protector taught me the truly brave man is not one who does not feel fear. He is the one who feels fear but goes forward in spite of it. That is why I have defended Bruhn so." He reached out to her, grasped her hand and pulled her to him.

Catryn allowed her head to rest on his shoulder with relief. She felt a lightness sing through her whole being.

"I should have trusted you, Dahl. The Elders advised me wisely." She saw Dahl begin to form a question, but forestalled it. There was no time for explanations now.

"I felt the evil in that man, Dahl," she said, stepping back and looking up at him. "I recognized it—recognized him. Even though he did not speak, I know his was the voice that I heard in my vision."

"What, then, does he want with Bruhn?"

"I do not know," Catryn answered. "But I doubt Bruhn's power to withstand him."

This time, Dahl did not argue.

Catryn chose to ride by herself that morning, following the others. So it was that when the wind sprang up behind them, she was the first to feel it. She signaled to the horse to stop, but even before she did so, the horse tossed its head uneasily and rolled its eyes back. The dragonfire that slept within them seemed to waken. A now-familiar wave of evil enveloped her.

"Dahl!" She screamed the warning, but it was too late. Even as Dahl reined Magnus in and drew his sword, the sky was blotted out by a huge shape. Eyes burning even more fiercely than the horse's, a dragon bore down upon them. A tongue of flame licked out and scorched a tree beside Catryn, but the beast was heading for Dahl.

Without waiting for her command, the horse spread its wings and they were flying. Momentarily diverted, the dragon checked its flight. For a fleeting instant Catryn thought it was about to follow her, but it swerved and headed back toward Dahl.

Dahl raised his sword, braced for the attack. Magnus neighed in terror, but held fast under Dahl's control. Catryn's horse needed no guidance; it flew straight for the beast.

"Stop!" Catryn screamed at the dragon.

The cry was instinctive. She had no reason to believe the dragon would obey her—would even hear or understand her—but it whipped its massive head around at the sound of her voice.

Dahl took quick advantage. He rose in his stirrups, as high as he could, and slashed at the exposed soft spot in the underside of the dragon's throat—its only vulnerable spot. It was a glancing blow, but blood, black and viscous, welled up out of the cut.

The dragon shrieked, louder by far than Catryn's cry. Its head swung again toward Dahl, jaws agape. Teeth as long and as sharp as swords flashed, and smoke vomited forth from its throat.

"Stop!" Catryn screamed again. "Harm him not!"

The dragon rose back into the air with one mighty sweep of its wings. It pivoted to hover above Catryn. Its eyes blazed straight into her own. Catryn gathered every shred of power within herself, concentrated it and sent it out in a wave against the beast. She steeled herself for the torrent of flame she knew would come.

But it didn't.

Why should I not? The words invaded Catryn's mind, deep and sonorous, throbbing like some kind of awesome musical instrument.

Stunned, Catryn stared at the beast. The dragonfire dimmed. She could see its eyes clearly. They were large and dark, the flames simmering deep within them. *Who are you to command me?*

I am Catryn, daughter of Ethelrue. Catryn's mind

108

flashed the answer across the space between them.

And I am Caulda of Taun. Your king slew my child. Why should I not take my vengeance?

I will not have it! Catryn gathered even more force to her—more than she had ever known she possessed. She threw it out as a barrier, a curtain, between the dragon and Dahl.

The dragon reared high in the air as if struck by the impact. It hissed in fury.

He will not always have you to protect him.

The words burned into Catryn's mind as if truly made of fire. She clenched her teeth, clutched the horse's mane and willed herself to stay in control. The beast must not sense any weakening. Catryn began to shake. She sank deep inside herself, concentrating on the power within her, blotting everything else out. She *must* keep Dahl shielded!

Just when she thought she could hold out no longer, the fire within her mind was quenched. The dragon's eyes that held her own so unswervingly blinked, then flamed into brilliance again. The beast swerved in the air, high above her, banked and was gone.

Catryn collapsed onto the neck of the horse, drained of every particle of will. When it landed, she slid off its back. It furled its wings tightly against its shoulders, took a few small nervous steps, then shook its mane.

Dahl had dismounted and was standing as if rooted to the ground, staring into the sky where the beast had disappeared.

"But I slew it," he was whispering. "I *know* I killed it."

"It was her child you killed," Catryn replied. The words shook.

Dahl whipped around to face her. "Her child? How do you know? That beast was the dragon's *mother*? How could you possibly know that?" Then, only just fully realizing what had happened, he added, "Why did it not kill me? It could have—why did it not?"

"I know that because she told me," Catryn said. "She is Caulda of Taun, and she did not kill you because I did not let her. I threw a shield around you. She could not get through it."

"You can do that?"

"I can."

Dahl stared at her.

"Do we go on?" Bruhn's voice broke through to them. He had also dismounted and leaned against his horse as if for support. His face was pale.

"Of course," Dahl answered.

"What other choice do we have?" agreed the Sele. If it had been unnerved during the battle, it did not show it now.

Bruhn remained standing where he was, staring at them all. Catryn had no need to explore his mind to know what he was feeling.

"The village the boy told me about should be close by," Sele the Plump said, its voice breaking into the tension. "Should we not be getting on?"

CHAPTER 10

Catryn slumped on her horse's back. Her strength returned to her slowly. As they drew near to the village, however, strange feelings began to overcome her. Not the evil she had felt before. Instead, she felt as if her mind were slowing down, deadening. She looked around her for reassurance. They were riding through a pleasant wood, not unlike the woods she had known as a child in her own world. The trees were in full leaf and sunlight filtered down through them. The sky was blue; clouds skimmed past. Were it not for the inexplicable dread that was increasing with every step her horse took, she would have thought the scene full of peace and tranquillity.

But that is the problem, she thought suddenly. It is too tranquil. Too peaceful. She cast her mind ahead of them to the village.

Where was the normal bustle of people? Where was the usual buzz of minds?

They trotted their horses into the village and stopped at a well to replenish their water jugs. Catryn threw a blanket over her horse's withers to cover up its wings. A young woman came to the well to draw water also.

"Good morrow," Catryn said pleasantly as she dipped her jug into the water beside her.

The woman did not respond.

Thinking perhaps she had not heard her, Catryn repeated her greeting. The woman continued to ignore her.

She acts as if I am not here, Catryn thought. Is she deaf? But she is not blind—surely, she could at least return my smile?

As if she were totally alone at the well, the woman filled her bucket, turned and walked away.

Dahl and Bruhn knelt beside her then to fill their jugs as well and douse their heads. Catryn felt their presence immediately, Dahl's puzzled concern and Bruhn's resentment burning still, so strong it overrode any other feeling within him.

Hard upon that came the realization that she had not felt the woman's presence at all. There had been a curious emptiness in the air around her, even when the woman had stood right beside her. She gazed after the woman and sent a tendril of thought reaching out to her. The tendril encountered nothing.

Jugs filled and the horses' thirst quenched, the party led their animals along the track that led into the village center. It was filled with people. They walked about, intent on their own business. It looked like an ordinary, everyday village scene. But there was something amiss.

"It is very quiet," the Sele remarked. "No one seems to exchange words or greetings with anyone else."

"Nor did that woman reply when I spoke to her at the well," Catryn said.

"The boy, Norl, he spoke of a strange silence that fell upon the village after the beast had flown away, did he not?" Dahl asked.

"He did," the Sele answered.

Catryn furrowed her brow as she watched the villagers. She searched ceaselessly with her mind, but could not connect with these people at all. That was more than troubling, but something else was wrong as well.

"They have no shadows," she said. "The people have no shadows."

It was true. The sun shone down bright and hard upon the village square, and although the trees and buildings all cast long, dark images, the people moving about between them had no shadows at all.

"What does this mean?" Dahl asked.

Catryn cast her mind out again. She probed with it, trying with all her energy to send threads forth to meet the minds of the villagers, but to no avail. No matter how hard she tried, her searchings found nothing.

"The village is empty," she said finally, exhausted with the effort. "There is no one here."

"What do you mean?" Dahl exclaimed. "The square is full of people."

"No," Catryn answered. "No one is there at all."

"Impossible," Dahl insisted. He strode forward. Catryn and the others followed. As they walked through the square they greeted the people they passed. No greetings were returned. Nor did the people even try to move out of their way. Dahl became more and more irritated.

"This is more than strange," he growled finally. A man was walking toward him. Deliberately, Dahl stood in the man's path. The man walked straight into him, then corrected himself, and walked around and past him. Still, no word was spoken. "They do not see us!" Dahl exclaimed.

"They see nothing," Catryn said.

She led the way now, through the village and out the other side where well-tended fields of grain and vegetables lay stretched out before them. People were working in the fields. Some were weeding and watering, others were filling waiting carts with the harvested produce, but again all was being done in an eerie silence. They walked on past and came to an orchard. Plump, crimson fruit hung from all the branches. A boy came toward them, carrying a basket-full.

"May I have one?" Catryn asked, testing.

As if she had not spoken, as if she did not even exist, the boy passed her by, wordlessly. Knowing what she would find, but determined to try in any case, Catryn sought out his thoughts. There were none. There was nothing but a blank and terrifying emptiness.

They walked in and around the village for the rest of the afternoon, trying to find one person, at least, who would respond to them. It was useless. Finally, they mounted and rode out through the fields to where the forest began again on the other side and there made camp.

"I don't understand this," Dahl said. "What can have happened here? Why will these people not speak?"

"They cannot," Catryn answered slowly. "They are not there," she repeated.

"That is what you said before," Dahl said. "What do you mean?"

"Their bodies are there, Dahl," Catryn replied, "but their minds are not."

Whatever it was that they faced, it was more powerful by far than she had imagined. For the first time, she allowed her mind to dwell on the possibility of failure. What if she could not protect Dahl? What if he were killed? And she? She could not die, she knew that—but she could be maimed. As the Protector had been. Maimed for life, for eternity! Horror, black and heavy, crept through her.

Help me! she cried silently to the Elders. But this time, when she so needed to hear, when she was ready to hear, there was no answer. She was beyond their reach.

They were on their own then, she and Dahl. And the Sele.

And Bruhn.

The night that followed was worse by far than any Catryn had ever known. They repaired to the woods on the outskirts of the village and made camp, but she refused the stew that Bruhn made, refused to speak even to Dahl. Instead, she sat hunched against a tree, lost within herself. She was barely aware of the others as they ate and settled down for the night, but they, too, made their preparations in silence—as chilled as she with what they had seen. There was some force at work here beyond all understanding.

She watched the moons rise, then watched them wane. Slivered crescents now, not the full orbs they had been when she and the others had set out from Daunus. Finally, while everyone slept, she rose, stiff and cold through to the marrow of her bones. She needed an escape. She shifted. A sleek, sinewy silver cat this time, as ethereal as the moons themselves. She shut her eyes and drew the blackness of the night into herself deeply. The world that was closed to her in human form unfolded itself to her senses. Welcomed her. She let herself sink into it until almost every semblance of humanity was banished from her mind, then she loped off into the darkness.

All night, she roamed. Through the forest, up hills and down into valleys. Avoiding always the habitations of humans. She could not bear the sight or smell of humans right now.

With the dawn she returned. Reluctantly, she shifted back into her own form, but something within her had been assuaged. The horror was not gone, but it was under control.

She was suddenly aware of a raging hunger, but even greater than that was the need to return to the village, to see again those husks that walked like people. She gulped down a handful of raw grain from the saddlebags of the Sele, then prepared to leave. She would not wait for the others. She would be back before they awoke. In any case, if Dahl did waken before her return, he would know she had only gone to investigate further and would soon be back. But, as she crept out of the camp and set her feet on the path to the village, a slight noise startled her. She whirled to find Sele the Plump at her heels.

"I will go with you," it said.

She met its eyes and knew that it understood the feelings that were driving her. The need that would not let her wait.

"Shall we ride?" it asked.

"No," she answered. "Not this time." She beckoned it to follow and they made their way out of the camp.

As soon as they were out of sight of the camp, Catryn stopped and laid her hand on the Sele's arm. "I know the people in the village seem not to see us," she said, "but I would go more inconspicuously anyway. Pause a moment." She twitched, shook herself and became a cat again. A small gray cat, almost as unsubstantial as a ghost.

The Sele stared for a moment, then a smile spread slowly over its face, surprisingly sly for a Sele. "Wonderful," it breathed. "And I, too, can disguise myself, although it is not a thing that we would ever let any other human see us do." He dropped to all fours. Face turned down to Catryn, his ears, normally held flat to his head, pricked up. A tail uncurled itself from where it had been hidden underneath the smooth fur.

The gray cat looked up at a gray image of itself, only bigger.

Wonderful indeed! Catryn thought.

Shall we be off, then? To her surprise, the Sele had heard her thought. And she had heard its unspoken reply!

So they, too, could communicate without voiced

words, at least in these forms. Good. That might be useful. She gave a quick nod and side by side, like two gray wraiths, they slipped along the trail to the village.

The villagers were just beginning to stir as Catryn and the Sele padded softly into the square. At first, Catryn kept to the shelter of some bushes, but soon did not bother—no one noticed either the small cat or the larger one. Carts were coming in from the fields, heavily laden with produce. The villagers began to line up beside the well at the center of the square. Catryn and the Sele settled themselves down to watch.

The carts pulled up. One by one the villagers went and received a small bag of vegetables and fruit. When they were finished, one cart was still more than half full of food. The man in charge of it spurred his horses on and started back out of the village.

Where does this food go? Catryn mused. Somehow she was certain that if she could find out, she might be closer to solving this puzzle.

Are you going to follow it? the Sele asked, glancing skyward with a worried look.

Yes, definitely, Catryn answered, but she looked up, as well. The sun was rising; it was getting late. She sent her mind back to their camp and sensed Dahl awakening, but she *had to* find out more here. As if pulled by a magnet, she began to lope along behind. After a moment's hesitation and another anxious glance at the sun, the Sele followed.

The cart rumbled slowly on. It lumbered around a bend in the path and was momentarily lost to sight. Catryn and the Sele sped up to follow it; then, as they also rounded the bend, they both stopped.

The man had pulled the cart up in the middle of the path. He sat in it, not moving, staring straight ahead. The horse lowered its head and began to graze on a patch of stubbly grass.

He is waiting for something, Sele the Plump whispered into Catryn's mind.

Or someone, Catryn responded. A strange sensation was beginning to stir deep inside her. A pulling. As if some force were acting upon her, drawing her to it. She left her place of concealment and slipped closer to the cart.

I like this not . . . the Sele began.

Catryn could feel the power drawing her on more and more strongly—it was almost impossible to resist. She reached the cart. At that moment the air in front of it began to shimmer and shift. An opening began to appear.

A portal!

There was no time to think. Catryn leaped into the cart.

Catryn! No!

The Sele's warning came too late. Nor could she

have heeded it. The cart moved forward, almost as if it, too, were being drawn through the quivering opening. At the last possible moment, Catryn felt a thump as Sele the Plump landed beside her.

Hide yourself! Catryn sent to the Sele.

They burrowed down amongst the fruit and vegetables, dirt and leaves, until they were completely hidden. There was a moment of silence— breathlessness—then the cart clattered over what felt like cobblestones and came to a halt. Catryn heard someone giving orders. It had been so long since she had heard voices that it startled her.

"Wait here," a man ordered, presumably to the driver of the cart. "We will unload later."

Silence descended again. Nothing moved. There was a noise that sounded like boots scuffling off. Catryn could not see the Sele but she could sense its presence near her. She sent a thought to it.

The guards are not mindless slaves. And the villagers obey their commands—we must take care!

She waited another few moments.

I think it is safe to get out now, she sent finally. She squirmed up through the vegetables, then sneezed. For a moment she froze. The Sele, who had emerged beside her, froze as well. The broad back of the villager who drove the cart was almost beside them, but he did not stir. Catryn sneezed again. She couldn't help it. Her nose was full of dirt, and bits of vegetation were tormenting her whiskers. She gathered herself together and leaped up over the side of the cart, trusting that there would be something more or less soft on the other side.

She landed lightly on grass. The Sele was not far behind, but the roundness of its substantial body made its landing much less graceful.

"Whoof!" it puffed aloud.

Again, they froze, but there was still no indication from the villager that he had heard them. He, obviously, was one of the silent ones. She sent out a cautious thought to determine if the guard was still around, but as far as she could tell there was no sentient human being near them at all.

Only then did she raise her head to see what lay before them.

The forest on this side of the portal was dark and looming. Mosses dripped from the trees like ropes of tears. The very air around them seemed heavy with despair. Catryn felt as if a shroud had been thrown over her mind. There was something . . . something warning her. Something she needed to remember . . . Instinctively, she cast out to Dahl, but the seeking tendril was brought up short, as if it had encountered a barrier.

The portal. She could not see through the portal with her mind. For a moment she was overwhelmed. A loneliness such as she had never felt before enveloped her. She was cut off from the Elders—and now cut off from Dahl.

The Sele must have sensed her feelings. *This is not good, Catryn. We must return to Dahl.*

Its thought came strongly through to her, more perturbed than she had ever known a Sele to be. But she could not heed its warning. The same force that had compelled her to cross through the portal was compelling her still. She peered through the trees. The outline of a building—a palace—loomed darkly through the low-lying mist. Dimly, she could make out stone walls and dark towers. Why was that so familiar to her? She tried to make sense of what she was seeing, but her mind was clouded, slow and heavy. She could not think.

She began to move toward the palace. Quickly, before the guard returned.

No, Catryn! There was an urgency now in the Sele's thought. *We must return to Dahl!*

Catryn heeded him not. She hardly heard him. Stronger, much stronger, than his plea was a silent voice calling to her from that grim citadel. She quickened her pace. She knew that voice. She *must* go to it.

She thrust the Sele out of her mind.

She broke through the trees into a cleared patch of land just in front of the looming walls. A massive door at the top of a stone staircase was flanked by two windows, which didn't show the slightest hint of light behind them. As Catryn looked, the door swung open.

She had to go in.

She did not hear the Sele's cry of warning as she padded up the stairs and through the door. She was in a long, narrow hallway. A guttering candle gave a scant, flickering light. In its glow she saw the bent figure of a man coming toward her. A man in a flowing cape. Not hooded now, but in the pall of this narrow vestibule all she could see of his face were two glittering eyes.

The door thudded shut behind her.

"Welcome, Catryn, Seer of Taun. I have been expecting you."

With those words Catryn's mind cleared as if swept by a wind. It was the voice of her vision. These were the walls she had seen. And she was within them. She had let herself be trapped! She tensed to spring, but before she could move, a hand swept down and scooped her up. She struggled with every ounce of energy she had. She spat and hissed and unsheathed tiny daggers of claws. She heard the man draw in his breath with an oath. Fierce joy filled her as she realized she had drawn blood. She redoubled her efforts, turning herself into a small, writhing fury. Still to no avail. For a second she thought of returning to her own form, then just as quickly decided against it. She would have a better chance of escape as a cat, she was certain of it, but then she heard the man shout, "The sack! Throw me that sack!"

The next moment Catryn was enveloped in a foul-smelling, rough-textured bag. It was small—so small she would never fit in it if she shifted back to her own body now. It was too late. Frantically, she sent her mind streaking out to the Sele.

I've been captured, she screamed silently. *Go for help!*

But could the Sele hear her? Before she could call again she felt the sack thrown down hard onto the stones. The world dissolved into blackness.

CHAPTER 11

The first thing Catryn realized when she regained consciousness was that her head hurt. Instinctively, she went to rub it with her hand, then remembered she was still in cat form. She must have made some small movement, though.

"So, you are awake, are you?" It sounded as if the man were speaking from across the room. Catryn could picture him sitting there, staring at the bag in which she was trapped, waiting for her to revive.

She froze.

"I have been watching you, Catryn, ever since you

left Daunus. But you know that, don't you?"

Catryn stayed as still as she could. Her mind was working furiously. She could not shift back to her own body as long as she was in the sack. And as long as she was in cat form, the full use of her powers was denied to her. She could not fight this man. She must get out somehow. Once out, surely she would be able to thwart him. She had controlled a dragon, had she not?

Her captor laughed. "You would like that, wouldn't you? But I am not such a fool as to give you the chance. I have you just where I want you, and that is where I intend to keep you."

He had read her mind! Even as the realization swept over her, he laughed again and the voice continued. The words were arrogant and sneering.

"Yes, I know what you are thinking. Have known ever since you left Daunus. It was amusing to watch you and Dahl make your plans. So sure of yourselves, weren't you?"

For a moment Catryn raged, then she controlled herself. She must concentrate on masking her mind. He must not be allowed to see into it.

"Well done, Seer of Taun," the man said as she closed her mind to him. "You learn quickly. But it will do you no good. Not unless you cooperate with me."

What do you want? Catryn threw the words out of her own mind at him.

"Much," was the reply. "Oh, yes. I want much! And you will help me achieve it."

Never!

"Do not be so quick to refuse me. You do not know what I have to offer you."

Then tell me, Catryn sent back. *Let me out of this bag and tell me.*

"That I will not be so unwise as to do," was the answer. "But I would talk with you." He was silent for a moment. "I have it," he said. "I know what we shall do."

She heard sounds as if the man were searching around. What sounded like boxes and pieces of furniture being moved.

Finally the man spoke again. "Ah, here it is. I knew it was somewhere around here." Fingers began to fumble with the knot that sealed the bag.

Catryn tensed every muscle in her body. When the bag was open ... The moment she saw a glimpse of light ...

She had no chance. A hand reached through the opening as soon as the knot was untied, but the other hand kept the opening wrapped tightly around the first. Catryn drew back as far as she could. The hand groped for her. She darted her head forward and bit. Her teeth closed on the soft patch of skin between thumb and forefinger.

The man cursed. The hand jerked back. Then it reached for her, grabbed her roughly by the neck before she could bite again and pulled her out.

Now! If she could just change back into human form! But before she could even begin to gather her power, she was stuffed into yet another prison. This time she found herself in a cage made out of twigs and branches. A cage such as a bird would be kept in. Bigger than the bag, with a bit more room for her, but still nowhere large enough for a person's body. Frustrated, Catryn whirled to face her captor, arched her back and spit.

"Spit and hiss all you want. It will do you no good." The face of her captor bent down toward her, smiling, tantalizingly close. She could see now that he was old. Lines were etched around a mouth that was drawn and cruel.

Catryn lashed out with a paw, all claws bared.

He pulled back with another oath. "If you would stay alive, Catryn, stop resisting me!"

Catryn stared, suddenly recognizing him. *Launan! You are Dahl's uncle!* The man who had put the Usurper in Dahl's place as a baby! Who had been the instrument of the forces of evil that had allowed the Usurper to enslave all of Taun.

"Yes," he sneered. His mouth twisted with bitterness. "That is who I am. The one who gave the Usurper—as you call him—his power. And in so doing I lost mine." He glared at Catryn. "He betrayed me. Would have destroyed me, but now I am even more powerful. To be feared even more."

Catryn stared at him. Was this really the sick, dying man she had seen but once before, when Dahl had discovered him chained and starving in the dungeons of the Usurper's palace?

"Oh, yes, Catryn, I am."

In her astonishment she had opened the door of her mind again.

"There is a force in this land that is mightier than you can imagine, Seer though you might be, Catryn of Taun. Mightier even than the Elders who support you. That force empowered me when I stole Dahl's kingdom from him, and that force has seen fit to use me again. Wizened and bent I may look to you, but you are no match for me, Catryn. You never will be! And I shall destroy Dahl."

But why? Dahl spared you. He set you free. Why should you seek to kill him?

"Spared me?" He fairly spat the words out. "For what? For a life of poverty and toil? I want much more than that!"

What, then? What is it that you want?

Launan spun away from her, took two paces, then whirled back. His face was contorted with wrath.

"Revenge!" he cried. "I want my revenge, and I have been plotting it for every single moment of these past three years. I have thought of nothing else."

Revenge on Dahl? Catryn still did not understand. *Dahl did you no harm.*

"Not Dahl! Not revenge on your weakling of a king. But revenge on the one I made powerful. The one who repaid me with torture and imprisonment. The one who lives still deep within your king. And if I must destroy Dahl in order to destroy him, so be it."

The Usurper!

"Yes."

She had left her mind unguarded again. She cloaked it hurriedly. Launan did not seem to notice. He began to pace again, almost in a frenzy.

"The one you call the Usurper will feel the flames of my wrath. He will pay for what he did to me. He will watch through the eyes of your king as I conquer his villages one by one and enslave his people—far, far more effectively than he did. They will serve *me* now, and he will watch, helpless to stop it. Finally, Daunus itself will be mine. Only then, when he has seen the extent of my triumph, will I destroy him. I will let the beast who obeys my commands have him. She burns for revenge against your king for slaying her child. She will kill him and in so doing kill them both. Then my revenge will be complete."

Catryn fought to think, yet not let Launan see her thoughts. She must warn Dahl—but what could she do? How could she escape?

Launan stopped his pacing and came to stand in front of Catryn's cage. His face calmed, became sly. He looked at her appraisingly, then spoke again. "Think you that Dahl can control the evil within him, Catryn? Do you not fear that the Usurper will eventually find a way to regain his power? Have you not worried about this?"

Unbidden and unshielded, the vision of Dahl's dragon scar, scarlet and angry, filled Catryn's mind. How often had she seen it flare when the Usurper stirred within Dahl? How often had she seen the

Usurper himself peer out at her from Dahl's own eyes. And how often had she drawn back, afraid in spite of herself of that hidden evil?

Launan leaped upon her unguarded thoughts.

"You see? You do doubt him! Dahl *must* die, Catryn. It is the only way to slay the Usurper. Abandon Dahl while you can. Help me and we will assure the future of Taun. *This* is the way."

Catryn thrust the doubts out of her mind and threw up the cloak again, but it was too late. She had let Launan see her most secret, hidden fears. Fears she had not even acknowledged to herself. But they were groundless, she knew that! She knew well that Dahl could live with the fate he had chosen. Dahl's struggle had taught her that a whole being is, of necessity, evil as well as good. As was she herself.

I have faith in Dahl, she told herself fiercely. I *do* trust him. The Usurper will never win over him. And he has the sword. The one weapon that will kill Launan.

She returned Launan's challenge with a glare.

Never! She sent all the fury she could summon streaking toward him. *I will never abandon Dahl!*

"You have already abandoned Dahl," Launan answered. "You abandoned him the moment you left him alone. And there is nothing now that you can do about it."

With that he left.

The room in which Catryn was imprisoned was dank and dark. A small slit of a window high above let in only a sliver of light. When Launan left, carrying his candle with him, the shadows took over. Then, finally, even that small amount of light faded, and Catryn realized night had fallen. Launan did not return. A maidservant came in and thrust a few bits of meat and a small dish of water between the cage bars. But when Catryn tried to reach the girl's mind she found only emptiness. The nothingness of the girl terrified her. What power was it that stole the very essence of these people? She ignored both the food and water and circled the small confines of the cage frantically, her thoughts bent on escape. She gnawed on the bars of the cage, but the twigs and branches were fashioned from wood as hard as iron—her small teeth could not make a dent in them. There was a latch, but it was securely fastened on the outside; besides, her cat paws could not possibly open it. Then she forced herself to sit and she conjured up every unbinding spell she had ever learned, but all to no avail. Either they would not work while she was in cat form or, and this last was a frightening thought, Launan had binding spells far stronger than hers.

When she tried to cast her mind throughout the

palace she found she could not. So Launan was powerful enough to block her in that way, too. In desperation, she tried again to summon the Elders, even though she knew it was useless. She was far beyond their reach now. Had Sele the Plump heard her cry for help? Had he been able to return to Dahl? What if he had not? Launan's words tormented her. She had to warn Dahl, tell him what she had learned—but how could she?

She had left him. She had allowed herself to be captured.

She had failed him.

Then, the next morning, the door to the room in which she was kept opened again.

"I have a surprise for you, my puss." It was Launan.

Catryn sprang to her feet. She started to arch her back defiantly, then shock flattened her down onto the floor of the cage. Unbelievingly, she stared at the heavily cloaked figure who had entered the room just behind Launan.

"I see you recognize our new friend," Launan said. "Will you not greet him nicely?"

Bruhn!

Bruhn looked at her, a puzzled look upon his face.

She sent a questing tendril toward him. His mind was there, she could feel it, but clearly he did not hear her.

"He does not recognize you," Launan smirked. "Indeed, how could he be expected to? A scruffy, bedraggled, sorry-looking specimen such as you bears little resemblance to the proud Seer of Taun."

"Is this really she?" Bruhn's voice was unbelieving.

"It is. Do you see now what I told you? The Seer of Taun has no power here. It is as I promised you—Dahl's quest is hopeless. You do well to throw in your lot with me."

What do you mean? What is going on here? How did you take Bruhn prisoner? Catryn sent her thoughts searing out to Launan.

"Oh, but he is not a prisoner, are you, Bruhn? He came here quite readily. He knows which side is the winning one—a clever young man such as he is."

Catryn felt something die within her. This was what she had feared, but never really believed, would happen.

"How can I know for certain that is Catryn?" Bruhn asked Launan. He was holding himself stiffly, with a kind of defiant arrogance, but his voice was taut with strain. "It looks like the most ordinary of cats to me."

Catryn stared straight into Bruhn's eyes. She yowled. A piercing, furious caterwaul.

Bruhn's pose faltered. He dropped his eyes. Good. He recognized her all right. Oh, if only Dahl had paid heed to her warnings!

"Catryn it is," Launan said with a laugh. "And she is not thinking very pleasant thoughts about us."

"You can hear her thoughts?" Bruhn asked.

"I can. Perhaps it is just as well you cannot." He draped his arm around Bruhn's shoulders.

Bruhn looked at Catryn from within Launan's embrace. He tried to smile, but his lips twitched. His eyes darted back and forth between her and Launan.

"And there is more," Launan said, his voice triumphant. "Show her, Bruhn, show her what you have brought to me."

Bruhn stepped away from Launan and threw back his cloak. Around his waist he wore Dahl's scabbard. Even as Catryn watched, he drew forth the sword. Dahl's father's sword. Horrified, Catryn heard the Elder's words echo in her mind: "Beware, it can be used for evil as much as for good." He faced her, his stance bold, but his eyes slid away from her appalled stare.

No! It was a scream within Catryn's mind. She could not even try to hide it. *Not Dahl's sword! Now Dahl is truly defenseless!*

"True, Catryn," Launan gloated. "Oh, so very true. Why else do you think I have been tempting Bruhn to betray you? And when you left Dahl you opened the way for me. It was easy to work on him then. Convince him that Dahl had forsaken him for you. Convince him to bring Dahl's sword here to me. Dahl is doubly lost, Catryn. That sword is the only weapon that can slay me. And now it is mine."

As if hypnotised, as if he had heard only the last words, Bruhn turned quickly to Launan. "You said it would be mine!"

"And so it shall, my son. When Dahl is dead."

Bruhn grimaced for a moment, as if with a stab of pain, but Launan spoke again quickly.

"You shall have the sword, my son, and you shall have power greater than Dahl could ever know. No longer the servant, *you* shall be the lord. You shall have what is rightfully yours." He turned to face Catryn.

"As for you, Catryn, you shall die," he said. "I gave you a chance and you refused it. I have no need of you now. Now that I have the sword of Taun in my possession, no one—not even Dahl—can harm me."

You cannot kill me, Catryn shot back desperately. *I am immortal. I cannot die!*

"Your body may not die, but what of your mind, Catryn?" Launan laughed.

Catryn felt herself shrivel. Desperately, she shielded her mind from him.

"Shield yourself as you may," Launan gloated. "It will do you no good. I have many ways of murdering your mind, Catryn. We will explore them together, you and I."

He turned back to Bruhn. "And when I have finished with her, I will go forth again and you will accompany me. Then you will see the extent of my power—the extent of the power that will be yours, as well."

Bruhn's hand tightened convulsively on the sword's hilt. "Where do we venture? To Dahl . . . ?"

Catryn could see the weapon tremble in his grasp. His knuckles grew white.

"No, not yet. First we make another foray and you will accompany us on it."

"Us?" Bruhn repeated.

"Myself," Launan answered, "and the creature that does my bidding. We have one more village to acquire—the village of a boy who interests me particularly. I almost had him once, but he escaped. This time I will find him. Then it will be time to take Daunus itself, and I will make an end to all this. Dahl will die and with him the one who betrayed me." His words were as hard and implacable as stone, but his eyes glittered with a hatred so intense it was almost joy.

Bruhn paled.

Good, Catryn thought. Let him feel fear. Let him realize what he has done. With whom he has allied himself. And what the dangers are therein!

Launan reached out a hand to Bruhn. "Give me the sword," he commanded.

Bruhn unbuckled the scabbard and held the sword out to Launan. Launan reached for it, then gasped and jerked his hand back. His eyes went wide with shock. Catryn could see a red welt rising where Launan's flesh had met the steel of the weapon.

He could not touch it!

Bruhn stared at him, confused, but Launan recovered himself quickly. He hid his hand within the folds of his gown and regained his composure.

"Wait," he said, as if nothing had happened, as if a thought had only just occurred to him. "I have a better idea." He gestured with his unburned hand toward a chest that sat against the farther wall. "Let the sword rest here tonight where Catryn can see it and reflect on her failure. The sight of it, so near and yet so completely out of her reach, will torment her more than anything else that I could devise. A fitting reward for scorning me. Let her see the visible proof of what her pride has cost her."

"It is no more than she deserves," Bruhn said, summoning up a defiance Catryn could not believe was real. "She turned Dahl against me."

Not true! Catryn raged. *You did it yourself! You have no one but yourself to blame for Dahl's loss of faith.*

But Bruhn could not hear and Launan merely laughed.

Then Bruhn spoke again. "Is it wise to leave the sword here?" he questioned. "If you cannot touch it, I could guard it . . ."

Launan fixed him with a cold, hard stare. "Do you dare think this sword has power over me?" he demanded.

"No . . ." Bruhn stumbled over the word. The air of confidence he had been assuming was suddenly shaken. "Of course not. I was mistaken. I must have been."

"You were. Now do as I bade you. Catryn can do naught but look at it and despair. She is helpless."

Bruhn placed the sword and scabbard carefully on the chest.

"Look long and look well, Catryn," Launan gloated. "It is the price of your defeat." With that, Launan threw his arm once more across Bruhn's shoulders and led him out of the room. Catryn stared after them. The anger and the defiance drained out of her. Launan was right. She was helpless and Dahl was alone. She did not even know if the Sele had managed to return to him. It could be dead. Unbidden, the memory of the Usurper's followers killing Sele for sport and eating them returned. If Sele the Plump had been caught in his own form by Launan's guards, they would have thought him no more than an animal. They would have made sport of killing him. They might already have feasted on him.

The horror she thought she had conquered returned to flood over her. They had lost. Taun was lost! Her stomach clenched and she retched. If a cat could weep, she would have wept.

CHAPTER 12

Shadows fell; the room darkened. Catryn barely noticed, so overwhelmed was she by her grief. Only gradually did she notice that the darkness was not complete. Indeed, it seemed to be lessening. Surely the night could not have passed without her noticing? She raised her head and looked around. The blackness outside the slit that served as a window was total, but the room was illumined as if with candles. She looked again and saw the sword, lying on the chest. It was glowing. The light from it seemed to pulse and radiate a kind of warmth that she could feel touching her, awakening her senses.

In an instant she was fully aware and concentrated on the weapon. There was more than warmth emanating from it. She could feel a magic, too. As she stared, she could feel enchantment entering her, filling her. Her powers were being returned to her, even in this cat form! She closed her eyes and sent an unbinding spell spinning into the lock of her cage, then waited, hardly daring to breathe. It sprang open. She was out in a heartbeat. One shiver, and she was back in her own form. She paused only long enough to settle herself into her body, then she was across the room. She caught up the sword and the scabbard on which it rested. She buckled the belt around her waist, but the sword she kept in her hand at the ready.

Catryn crept across the room to the door. It was locked but that was no barrier now. She unlocked it with an almost casual wave of her hand, then opened it as quietly as she could and slipped out into the passageway beyond. A sudden wild notion thrust itself into her mind.

Launan! With this weapon she could find him and kill him herself. And then—Bruhn. The thought of revenge was sweet and heavy. Enticing. She looked down the hall. Where, in this vast palace, would Launan have his rooms? She sent an exploratory tendril out. But, as she searched, another faint awareness pricked back to her along her thread. A stirring. She drew back her probe in an instant.

Launan! Of course, he would feel her seeking. Had she alerted him? She held her breath, trusting to her ears alone now to warn her of danger. She must get away! Get out of the palace as quickly as she could— return the sword to Dahl. The sword was his; it was he who would wield it to slay Launan. What Bruhn's fate would be she did not know, nor could she think on it now.

She turned the other way, certain somehow that this was the path to her freedom. Cautiously, Catryn made her way through the gloom. The sword glowed now but faintly, only enough to show her the way. She watched for guards, tentatively sent her mind ahead of her to ensure there was no danger, but she found nothing. How sure Launan was of his power that he felt no need for guarding here!

Fear rose within her. Launan's presence loomed everywhere. She came to the end of the hallway and paused. Two more passageways led off from it in opposite directions. Which one to take? Her desire for haste made her frantic. It was only with the greatest of efforts that she calmed her mind enough to seek the proper direction. Still, she must guard it carefully. She could not let Launan sense her seekings.

Finally she turned a corner and there, in front of her, was the hall and the door through which she had entered. With a last quick glance around her, she darted across and put her hand to the latch. It did not give under the pressure, nor did it respond to her unlocking spell. A very strong magic must be guarding it. For a moment panic threatened to overwhelm her yet again, then she gathered herself together. She would use the power of the sword, as well as her own. She touched the door with the shining blade and sent the most powerful of the unlocking spells she had learned through the weapon and into the ancient wood of the portal. Soundlessly, it swung open.

Once outside, Catryn forced herself to wait in a dark alcove and take stock of her situation. She sheathed the sword and hid it under her cloak. Only then did she allow herself to move forward. Keeping to the shadows, she circled around the palace until she found the cobblestoned road. The silence here was almost as profound as the silence beyond the portal to the domain of the Elders, but here it was a threatening, uneasy silence. She allowed herself to breathe more freely when she reached the shelter of the trees, but still was careful to keep hidden until she judged she must be near where the cart had come through. She set herself to searching for the portal with her mind. She found it, but then sensed something else as well. Dahl and the Sele—they were here! On this side of the portal!

"Dahl?" she called softly. "Sele? Where are you?"

A bush rustled, leaves parted. Dahl stepped out of hiding, closely followed by Sele the Plump.

"Catryn!" Dahl cried. "Thank all that is good in this world that you escaped!"

"Did you hear me, then?" Catryn asked the Sele. "When I was captured?"

"Yes," it answered. "I heard you. I knew there was nothing I could do here, so I made haste to return to Dahl to seek his aid. We have been planning as to how to reach you."

"Is . . ." Dahl's voice, usually so strong and sure, faltered. "Is Bruhn with you?"

"He is not," Catryn answered. "But we must not tarry here." She cast an anxious glance behind her. "Quickly, through the portal and we will talk then."

She began to make the opening. One by one, they slipped through. Only then, in the light of their own familiar twin moons, did she see Dahl's face. It was the face of a man ravaged by hurt. She reached out to him.

"Bruhn has betrayed us," Dahl said. "Even as you warned, Catryn. But worst of all, he stole the sword of Taun while I slept. I rejoice that you have escaped, but our quest is doomed. Taun is doomed. Without that weapon I cannot fight."

Catryn unclasped the fastening of her cloak and let it fall to the ground. Dahl stared as she unbuckled the heavy belt and held out sword and scabbard to him. The sword glowed no longer, but it reflected the moons' light in sharp-edged, silver shards.

"I could not return Bruhn to you, Dahl, but I have brought your sword."

"How . . . ?"

Quickly, she recounted all that had transpired. When she finished talking, Dahl sat silent for a long moment, his head bowed.

"I would have sworn upon my own life that Bruhn would never have betrayed me," he said finally.

"The blame is not all his," Catryn said. "Launan's power is great, so great that he entrapped me. How could he not lure Bruhn to him? It is my fault. The Elders enjoined me to help Bruhn; that I did not do. I let my anger at him cloud my judgment. And I should never have left you. If I had been there, Launan would not have been able to prevail upon Bruhn. I trusted too much in my own powers, Dahl. Launan said that it was my pride that caused my downfall and he spoke truth."

Dahl straightened. He fastened the sword once more around his waist. The dragon scar flamed. For one brief second Catryn saw the Usurper look out through Dahl's eyes, dark with fury. This time she did not quail. Dahl hooded his eyes and forced him back. His voice was flat and cold when he spoke again.

"If what you say is so, then Launan's own pride is by far the greater. And so much the greater shall be his downfall. I will speak no more of Bruhn. You say Launan intends to attack another village?"

"Yes," Catryn answered. Suddenly she remembered what Launan had said about "one particular boy" who had escaped him. Could he have meant Norl? He must have. But what was so special about Norl? She shook her head to clear it. There was no time to think on that now. "That is what he told Bruhn. I think he meant the village of that boy, Norl. After that he will take Daunus itself."

"Then Norl's village is where we must go."

The echoes of Launan's anger rang in Catryn's mind. She shuddered. How much greater would it be now? Now that she had escaped and taken with her the sword of Taun?

They began to retrace their steps and make as much haste as possible. Even so, Catryn had all she could do to keep from taking the horse and flying on ahead of Dahl and the Sele. She felt—she knew!—that speed was of the utmost importance. She remembered Launan's words and the glee with which he was planning the conquest of Norl's village. She could see Norl clearly, see the relief in his mother's face when at last he had been able to speak of what he had seen. But what would happen to the boy if his village was attacked and enslaved as the other village had been? What did Launan want with him? Launan *must* be stopped. She raged with impatience, but controlled it. She could not go on ahead. She would not leave Dahl unprotected again.

She cast her mind ahead of them, probing constantly, seeking out the mind bustle of the villages that lay ahead of them. Nowhere could she sense the empty numbness that characterized the conquered villages. So far, all seemed well. They were keeping ahead of Launan. She could even feel echoes of the Elders beginning to sing in her mind. They became stronger and stronger as they made their way south. With this she had to be satisfied.

They made their way around villages, preferring to make camp in the woods at night and hurry on as quickly as possible. On the morning of the third day they approached the boy's village. To Catryn's relief, the streets were full of people going about their business, bustling and noisy as usual. Catryn looked for Norl and his mother amongst them, but did not see them.

What to do now? There would be no way of knowing what the best defense would be until the danger was actually upon them. She cast her mind out to the north, then reeled with the sudden wind that raced to meet her. The danger *was* upon them! They had only just arrived in time!

"He's come!" she cried. "Launan is here!"

Barely had the words left her mouth when the scene before them was transformed. A shadow slipped between the villagers and the sun, then the dragon was upon them. People stopped, looked skyward and screamed. They scattered in panicked flight, but there was no escape. The dragon swooped down over the village square, then rose into the air again, trailing a ragged cloak of darkness behind her. Again and again she swooped. Over the square, over the houses. Every time she rose back into the sky she trailed a larger and larger latticework of darkness.

"Stay inside!" Catryn found herself screaming to the villagers. But, as if drawn out in spite of themselves, the people swarmed out of doorways and into the streets.

Catryn turned her mind to the dragon. She had stopped her once before—could she stop her again? She sent out a command with all the force she could muster, but all it encountered was swirling chaos. And then, an echo of cruel laughter. Launan! She could not see him, but he was here and the dragon was his creature, obeying only him. She cloaked her mind immediately—Launan must not know she was here—but not before she had sensed his rage. It was almost overwhelming.

Then she saw Norl. He was running down the village path toward the well. It seemed as if he were running to challenge the beast itself, but it was his mother he was trying to reach. Mavahn stood there, too shocked to move as the dragon swept down upon her.

Catryn did not stop to think. She kicked the horse with her heels and spurred it into a gallop. Beside her, she saw Dahl do the same. They tore after Norl. Catryn caught up to him just as the beast wheeled down. With a strength she did not know she possessed, she reached out, grabbed Norl by his tunic and hauled him up. Dahl reined Magnus in and drew his sword. Magnus reared up on his hind legs with a scream of defiance.

"Dragon!" Dahl shouted. "Do battle with *me!* I challenge you!"

But the dragon was fixed now on Catryn. And Norl. She banked and dove toward them.

With Norl lying half on and half off the withers of the horse, Catryn raced for the safety of the trees.

"Faster!" she cried to the horse, but Caulda was close upon them.

"Fly!" Catryn cried and tightened her grip on Norl.

The horse's wings unfurled with a thunderous clap. In an instant they were airborne. The dragon, burdened as she was by her plunder, could not follow. Her eyes blazed.

So the child is important to you, too.

The words seared into Catryn's brain.

Guard him well — if you can. You may have escaped me now, but I will have that child.

Catryn clutched Norl tightly. She heard him whimper in terror, felt him cling to her.

The dragon hung motionless for a moment, wings beating the air, then she swung her massive head around to glare at Dahl. *And I will answer your puny king's challenge then! He will not escape me, either.* With that she banked and climbed, higher and higher until she disappeared into the north, dragging her dark burden behind her in a sheet that blotted out the sky. The villagers milled aimlessly about. No one screamed. No one spoke. There was absolute silence. Mavahn still stood beside the well. She looked around her as if uncertain as to why she was there. Catryn guided the horse to a landing beside her. Norl leaped off before the animal had touched all four hooves to the ground.

"Mother!" he cried as he launched himself into her arms.

Mavahn looked at him with a puzzled, vacant look in her eyes. She didn't answer.

"Mother!" Norl insisted, his voice breaking.

Mavahn unwound his arms from around her and, without a word, walked down the path to their house. Norl ran after her. Catryn followed. As Mavahn reached the poor garden in front of her home, Norl grabbed at her yet again. She stared at him wordlessly and freed herself from his embrace. She went into the house and shut the door in his face.

Norl screamed and beat upon it with his fists. He was sobbing now with huge, body-wrenching gulps.

Catryn dismounted and ran to him. She tried to gather him in her arms, but he beat her off. Then, suddenly, he collapsed.

A voice spoke beside them.

"Norl, you must come with us now."

Catryn looked up to see Sele the Plump. It reached out a hand to Norl and helped him back to his feet.

"But my mother . . ." Norl began.

"We cannot help her here," the Sele said. "But come with us and we will find a way to bring her back. Your mother and all the others as well."

"You can do that?" Norl looked at the Sele with wide eyes, obviously wanting to believe.

"We can," the Sele replied. It was as calm as ever.

"And we will," Catryn promised, but although her words were fierce and defiant, her voice was ragged. They rejoined Dahl. He sat astride Magnus by the well, sword drawn still, his face as white as death. The dragon scar throbbed upon his cheek. His eyes were dark, bottomless holes. He breathed as heavily as if he had, indeed, done battle as he stared at the lifeless forms walking senselessly around the village square.

"I failed them," he said.

"Is this what happened in the village you saw, Norl?" Catryn asked. They had made camp in the woods, just inside the trees.

Norl, however, did not answer. The boy sat staring back at his village.

Catryn did not try to question him further. She could feel his pain. Knew he could not speak. She could feel Dahl's pain, too, cloaked now with an icy fury as he turned to her.

"The dragon did not kill them," he said. "But what did she do?"

"She stole their shadows," Sele the Plump said.

Both Dahl and Catryn stared at it.

"Look," the Sele said. "It is late afternoon. The shadows of the trees and houses are long. But the people cast no shadows. They are gone. You noticed that before, Catryn, but we did not realize the meaning of it then. Those shadows made up the dark cloud the dragon pulled behind her. She stole them. And with their shadows . . ." he paused. "And with their shadows, I think, she stole their souls."

Catryn felt a coldness enter into *her* soul. "That is why they are like empty husks," she said, the words no more than a whisper. She could hardly speak for the horror of it. "But where is she taking the shadows? What does she do with them?" This was an evil such as she could never have imagined.

"What does a dragon ever do with its hoard?" Dahl answered. He, too, looked shaken but his words were cold and hard. "She has taken them to her den. To sit on them and guard them as she would a treasure."

"And what greater treasure could she have," the Sele added, "than the souls of men and women?"

There was a long moment during which none of them could speak. Finally, Catryn found words.

"So that is how Launan enslaves them," she said.

"It would seem so," Dahl replied. "And I think I know where the dragon has gone. Remember the crevasse where you fell, Catryn, when we were first on our way to Daunus?"

"Yes," she answered.

"Remember how the Protector, in the form of a hawk, rescued you by grasping you in his talons and flying off with you?"

"I do," Catryn answered, gripping her arms at the remembered pain of those sharp, ruthless claws.

"What you did not know at the time," Dahl went on, "was that the reason for such haste in getting you out of there was because a beast just such as this one was emerging from the depths of that crevasse."

"The beast you slew?"

"The same one."

"The child of the beast we face today," Catryn said.

"So you said before," Dahl replied. "But how did she tell you? I heard no speech."

"I talked to her with my mind, and she to me," Catryn answered.

Sele the Plump nodded as if it had already guessed the truth. As it probably had, Catryn thought.

"I did not know you had that power," Dahl said.

"I did not know it either until then," Catryn said. She felt no reluctance now at allowing Dahl to see the truth.

"And she told you it was her child?"

"She did."

"If this dragon is, indeed, the mother of the one I slew," Dahl said, "then might she not live in the same den her devil child did?"

The Sele interrupted before Catryn could answer. "Dragons have always lived there," it said matter-of-factly. "They have been a constant nuisance to us."

"Then that is where we must go," Catryn exclaimed. "We must find her there. Destroy her before she attacks Daunus!" And before she destroys Norl, she added in her own mind.

"No. First we go to Daunus," Dahl said. "That is where Launan intends to attack next, is that not so, Catryn?"

"It is," Catryn answered. "But what more can we do there than we did here? If we can trap the dragon in her lair—get to her before she gets to Daunus . . ."

"No," Dahl repeated. "We must go to Daunus first. I cannot allow it to be taken."

"But without Caulda, Launan will not have the power to conquer Daunus," Catryn argued. Her voice rose. She *must* convince Dahl.

Sele the Plump interrupted them. "Dahl is right," it said. "And I think, perhaps, this is where my people can help."

Catryn made as if to argue further, but for once the Sele was adamant. "Trust me, Catryn," it said. "I will confer with my people and then meet you in Daunus. You must make haste to get there as quickly as possible. I do not think they are finished here yet," it went on, "and we can only hope that it will be a few days more before they attack again. That will give us time to get to Daunus before they do."

"But what is it your people can do?" Catryn asked. Every fiber of her being disagreed with the Sele, but even as she mustered more arguments she seemed to hear Tauna's voice. *Trust,* the Elder had said. But how could she when she was so certain it was a mistake? Or, whispered a small voice inside her, was this just her pride overriding her judgment again?

"I would prefer not to say just now," Sele the

Plump replied, unruffled as usual. "But I have a plan. I will leave at first light in the morning. You must get to Daunus as quickly as you can," it repeated.

"We will do that," Dahl agreed, and with that Catryn had to be satisfied.

"Will you go by horseback?" Dahl asked.

"No," the Sele answered. "I can travel more quickly on my own."

"How . . . ?" Dahl began.

"It can," Catryn answered, giving in to them. "I know that." She remembered how quickly and smoothly the Sele moved in its animal form. It would be much easier for it to slip through the forest that way than to follow the paths on horseback. And she—she could take the horse and fly. But what about Dahl and Norl?

"I can go ahead on the winged horse . . ." she began.

"*I* will take the horse, Catryn," Dahl said.

She bridled again and opened her mouth to challenge him. He forestalled her.

"Daunus is my city," Dahl declared. "It is I who must protect it. His face hardened; the dragon scar burned. "And this time I will not be taken by surprise. This time I will force the beast to do battle with me. If she would take my city as she took the others, she will have to kill me first."

This Catryn could not accept. "But you do not have the power to fight the dragon," she cried. "Only I can do that!"

"Not true, Catryn," Dahl replied. "I fought and killed one dragon. I can fight this one."

"But without me there to shield you . . ."

Dahl would hear no more. "I will send the horse back to you as soon as I arrive." The tone of his voice brooked no further argument.

"It is decided then," Sele the Plump said. Its words dropped like smooth, calm pebbles into the space between them. "But now it is getting late. "We can do nothing until tomorrow in any case." It began to rummage in its horse's saddlebags. "Now it is time for a good dinner. A good dinner always helps."

CHAPTER 13

The Sele curled up on its blanket soon after eating and was almost immediately asleep. Dahl followed suit. The boy would not eat, but he did curl up beside the Sele and he, too, seemed to sleep, but Catryn could not. Her mind would give her no peace. She felt control slipping from her. Things seemed to be going so wrong! Finally, she could lie still no longer. She rose quietly and stole away from the campsite to stand, staring at the village. The villagers were still stirring, walking mindlessly here and there, seemingly without purpose, even though it was now dark and late.

Something was different here, she thought as she watched them. This was not as it had been in the other village. There the people had been going about their business in the normal way, even though they had been taken over by Launan. They had been following their usual daily routines. Why was it not so here?

There must be something more going to happen, she thought. With that she drew her cloak more closely around her and set herself to waiting.

At dawn she sat there still. Nothing had changed in the village. Then, just as the sun was rising and the first cocks began to crow, she heard hoofbeats. She rose, stiff from the long sitting, and hastened to hide herself behind a tree.

A column of about twenty horsemen rode into the village along the road that led north. They rode in a strange kind of silence. There was none of the normal sounds of an army on the march. No harnesses jangled, no orders were given. Even the hoofbeats of the horses sounded muffled. As Catryn watched, they drew up in the village square, dismounted and tethered their horses, still without speaking. No orders were given. It was as if they were all so well rehearsed they had no need of commands.

As well it might be, Catryn thought, if this is what they do with every captured village.

The horsemen, or guards, if that is what they were, began to round up the people. Men and women obeyed them without resistance; children were as quiet and passive as their parents. After everyone who was out in the open was herded together on the small green in the village square, some of the guards began to search the houses. They made no attempt to knock at doors, but simply opened them, disappeared inside, and then reappeared either alone or with some person they had found within. Catryn held her breath as she saw them approach Mavahn's house. Two guards went inside. They left the door open. They returned, leading Mavahn, who followed them willingly.

The guards were making a selection. Some of the men and women were being led over to where the horses were tethered. There their wrists were bound and they were roped together. Catryn almost cried aloud when she saw Mavahn chosen. The guards who had selected the men and women to be taken remounted their horses. One, who looked like their leader, held the long rope to which the prisoners were attached. The rest of the guards encircled the villagers. All was done in the same eerie silence. Then everyone stood still. They seemed to be waiting.

Suddenly, Catryn could not see from where, a man's figure appeared. He stood before the villagers, his cloak billowing and blowing as if in a high wind, but the air was still. He spoke, finally breaking the silence. Catryn could not make out the words, but she recognized the voice immediately. It was Launan. She strained harder to hear what he was saying, but kept her mind well guarded.

He seemed to be giving orders, telling the villagers what they must do. They gave no signs of hearing him but, when he finished, they began to break off into groups. Many of the women returned to their houses. Some of the men began to hitch horses to carts; others took up implements and started for the fields that surrounded the village. As the sun rose higher, the village took on the appearance of the other captive village they had visited. All went about their normal routine, but nowhere was there any sign of vibrant life. They had become soulless slaves, as had the others. The rest of the guards now mounted their horses and rode off, leading the captive villagers. Catryn waited to see what would happen next.

A second figure appeared beside Launan. Bruhn! A laugh echoed across the space between her and the two figures. She could just make out Launan's voice.

"Did I not tell you," he said, "did I not tell you how easy it was? And even without the sword I will conquer Dahl. You will see!" The words were loud and defiant, but Catryn could hear the fury underlying them.

An equal rage began to rise within her, but she cloaked it carefully. Launan must not know she was here. She drew a deep breath and folded in upon herself. She lifted her head and drew in the scent. The scent of evil. Her eyes reflected back the light; sleek black fur gleamed. She padded softly and silently toward the two figures.

They did not see her. With every step her rage grew

stronger. She was not thinking now of anything but what these two had done. They must be punished. *They must be stopped.* She felt the growl in her throat, but suppressed it. She was almost upon them; their backs were turned. She gathered her muscles for the leap. Launan first, and then the traitor, Bruhn.

But in that instant Bruhn turned and saw her.

"Master!" he cried and threw out an arm to warn Launan.

Launan whipped around just as the wildcat jumped.

It was as if she had hit a wall. A wall of solid, unyielding stone. Catryn fell back, dazed. The trees, the sky itself seemed to collapse down upon her. The brightness of the dawning sun disappeared, replaced by blackness. It was only with the greatest effort of will that she held onto consciousness.

When she could see again, Launan and Bruhn were gone.

Catryn recounted to Dahl and Sele the Plump all she had seen. Dahl's mouth twisted as she told him of Bruhn's part in it, but he said nothing, only continued to make ready for his journey. As she watched him leap onto the horse's back and settle himself in behind its wings, she could not suppress her fear for him. He was going to battle and she was being left here. What would happen if she could not get to him in time? She glanced over to where Norl still lay curled up. If it were not for that boy, she thought, I, too, could be off. Like the Sele. I have the ability to travel quickly if I wish . . .

Of course! Of course, there was a way for her to get to Daunus—almost as quickly as Dahl, certainly as quickly as Sele the Plump. It would depend on the boy. On whether she could convince him.

"I'll send the horse back," Dahl began.

"No," Catryn said. "There is no need for that."

Dahl's eyebrows rose.

"I will go as a cat. I can travel swiftly that way," Catryn explained.

"And the boy?"

"He can ride me."

"Are you certain?" Dahl asked.

"Yes," Catryn answered. "It will be the quickest way."

Dahl seemed relieved. "You will come to the palace when you reach Daunus, then?"

"I will," Catryn said. "Be off, now. There is no time to waste."

Dahl looked at the Sele.

"I will go where I am needed," it said. "Do not worry if you do not see me."

Dahl hesitated a moment further, made as if to say something else, then changed his mind. He set his face toward the south and spurred the horse into the air.

After they had left, Catryn approached Norl. The fire had burned low and he was lying asleep as close to it as possible. She knelt beside him. She had assured Dahl the boy could ride her; now she must convince *him*.

"Wake, Norl," she said, rubbing his shoulder.

He opened his eyes. "Mother?"

"Your mother is safe, Norl," Catryn said. She could only hope she spoke truly.

Norl sat upright. "I must go to her!"

"That is not possible," Catryn said. "Trust me, Norl, we will save her, but for now we must go back to Daunus."

"To Daunus?" The boy was still befuddled. "Why must we go to Daunus?" He looked around him. "Where are the others? Where is the Sele?" His voice rose, at the edge of panic.

"They have gone on ahead," Catryn answered. "We must follow as quickly as possible."

Norl leaped to his feet. "I cannot leave my village!" he cried. "My mother will need me."

Catryn drew in her breath. "She is not here, Norl. Launan—he who controls the dragon—came and took her with some of the other villagers."

"Took her? Where?"

"Back to his palace, I imagine. She will be all right, Norl. I have been there. He makes the people work for him, but he treats them well. She will be safe, and after we have defeated him we will go back and set her free. I promise you, Norl," Catryn said. "But for now we must go to Daunus and stop Launan."

Norl looked at her, his eyes bright with tears.

"Did I not save you from the beast once?" Catryn asked.

"Yes," he replied, his voice small.

"Then you must believe that I will save your mother." Even as she spoke, Catryn felt the anger solidifying within her. She would do this. She *would* defeat Launan!

"This is what we must do," she said then to Norl. "And you must be brave." She watched the tears dry and his eyes widen with fear as she explained. "Can you do it?" she asked.

He nodded. The smallest of nods.

"You will not run away in terror when I shift?"

He shook his head from side to side. Again, the smallest of movements.

Catryn could only hope he would be able to keep his resolve.

"First we must take care of the horses," she went on, making her voice brisk. "We cannot just leave them here. Come, we'll find a stable in the village for them."

She took the boy by the hand and led him into the village. The townspeople went about their business as usual. They paid no attention to Catryn and the boy. When they came to the path that led to Norl's house, he stopped.

"There is a stable beside our house. A farmer uses it to store his grain," he said.

"Very good," Catryn answered.

They led the horses to the stable and pushed the door open. Inside it was warm and heavy with the smell of grain. Norl and Catryn found stalls and filled the mangers with fodder. Just as they finished, a figure appeared in the doorway.

"The farmer!" Norl whispered.

Catryn stared at him, momentarily nonplussed. Then she remembered how Launan had spoken to the villagers, commanding them. She placed herself directly in front of the man.

"You will care for these horses until I return," she ordered.

The man looked back at her, unresponsive, but he set about pitching more hay into the mangers.

"And bring water for them from the well," Catryn added.

The farmer turned, picked up a bucket, and made his way out of the stable and down the path to the well.

Norl looked after him, then turned to Catryn, puzzled.

"Catryn?"

"Yes?"

"That farmer—what ailed him?"

Catryn hesitated. There was no way to explain, however, except to tell him the truth.

"He has lost his soul, Norl. That is what the dragon does when she swoops down upon the people and steals their shadows. She steals their souls as well."

There was a silence, then he spoke again, his voice small.

"And my mother? Is that what happened to my mother?"

She could not lie to him. "Yes, Norl. That is what happened."

Another silence.

"What does the beast do with the souls?"

"We think she carries them back to her den and keeps them there."

Norl stared up at her, eyes wide. "When you save my mother, will you save her soul as well?" he asked.

Catryn looked back at him, and it seemed as if she were seeing into the clear blue sky itself. The look of trust on Norl's face was almost enough to break her heart.

"I will," she said.

CHAPTER 14

"You won't be afraid?" Catryn asked when they were once more within the shelter of the trees.

"I won't," Norl assured her. He looked apprehensive, but also a bit excited. "What will you look like? Will you be very big?"

"Yes," Catryn answered. "I will be big. I will look like the biggest cat you could possibly imagine. Almost as big as a horse. Remember," she added, "I will not be able to speak to you, so you must do exactly as I've told you. And I will be able to understand you, so you can talk to me."

"I'll remember," Norl answered. He nodded his head, his eyes bright.

Catryn was relieved. For the moment, anyway, he had ceased to fret about his mother.

"Stand there. Don't move," she ordered. She took a few paces away from him, then drew in her breath.

A shimmer in the early morning darkness of the trees, an instant when time itself seemed to pause—and an enormous lioness stood before Norl.

In spite of himself, he let out a cry and fell back. Catryn held herself still.

Come, Norl, she thought, even though she knew he would not hear her. *Don't be frightened.*

"But I *am* frightened," he said, his eyes fixed upon her.

Catryn froze. He could not have heard her.

"I thought you said you would not be able to talk to me," he said then.

You can hear me?

"Yes—I can hear you." A puzzled look came over his face. "But you're not talking, are you? How is it that I can hear you?"

You're hearing my thoughts, Norl. Well done, she hastened to add, to reassure him. *You must be a clever boy, indeed.*

"Hearing your thoughts? How can I do that?"

Catryn did not know the answer to that question. And she didn't have time, either, to think about it.

It will make things much easier, she sent her thoughts to Norl. *Get on my back now. We must be off.*

Norl looked at her apprehensively, then sidled up to her. Hesitantly, he put out a hand, but did not quite dare touch her.

Don't worry, Catryn encouraged him. *Climb up. I'll hold still for you.*

Norl took a deep breath. He grasped the fur at the back of her neck and pulled himself up. Catryn turned her head to look back at him. She could smell the fear on him, but he held himself steady.

Lean down and hold on tightly around my neck, Catryn told him. *I am going to run as fast as I can.*

She felt the boy's arms encircle her neck. He drew a quick breath, then took a firm hold.

Now, we go! She began to lope, slowly at first, but picking up speed as she felt the boy secure upon her back.

Keep your head down, she thought to him, then swerved off the path and into the trees.

Once she felt confident that Norl would not fall off, she let herself run full out. Dodging trees, avoiding obstacles by scent and by instinct, she almost forgot the reason for their haste and lost herself in the joy of movement. How free she felt in this form! She cast around continuously as she ran, but could detect no scent of evil.

They sped along in this manner until the sun had risen high above them. Norl had not said a word, nor had his grip slackened. When the warmth of the sun's rays began to streak stronger and stronger down through the branches of the trees, however, Catryn heard him speak.

"Can we stop?" he cried into her ear. "I don't think I can hold on any longer."

It was as if he had called her back from another world. She could have kept on forever, it seemed. Reluctantly, she slowed and then came to a halt under a tall tree that gave good shade. A stream trickled by at its foot. She realized suddenly that she was thirsty.

There's a stream here. Drink, she thought to him. She wondered for a moment if he would really hear her, or if she had just imagined it, but he slid down her back and ran toward it happily. She followed more slowly, then sank her muzzle into the water and drank deeply.

"I'm hungry," Norl said when he had assuaged his thirst.

There is bread and cheese in the pack you carry on your back, Catryn sent. As Norl bent to open it, she gathered into herself and returned to her own form. Norl jumped back, startled, then grinned.

"I like how you do that," he said. He bent back to the pack. "Do you want some of this?" he asked, holding out a fistful of bread and a chunk of cheese.

Catryn looked at it. She had not been able to bring much. It would have to do them until they reached Daunus. She calculated quickly. It had taken them several days to reach Norl's village from Daunus on their way north, but they had been traveling slowly. Still, it would be at least two or three days before they could get back to it. It would be best to save the food for Norl. She could forage for herself in her cat form.

"I'm not hungry right now," she answered. "I'll eat later."

After he had eaten and she had repacked his bag, she shifted back to her cat form. Norl leaped up on her back eagerly this time, twining his fingers firmly into the fur around her neck. She began to trot, then lengthened her stride.

Careful as she was, however, by the end of the second day there was only a crust of bread left and the rind of the cheese. Catryn worried for Norl. Then she remembered. When she and Dahl and the Protector had had need of food, the Protector had disappeared into the trees and returned with a marvelous fruit that had satisfied their hunger completely. Deliverance fruit, he had called it. Green and lumpy on the outside, but the flesh inside had been moist and cool, satisfying thirst as well as hunger. A magical fruit, he had said. It contained no seeds and could not be grown. He had refused to show Catryn where he had found it, however, saying only that if she were in need and had the necessary faith, she would find it.

"Wait for me here, Norl," she said now. "I will return in just a few moments."

Norl looked at her, worried. "Where are you going?"

"To find us food," Catryn answered. "Stay." Back in her own form now, she strode confidently into the bushes that surrounded their small campfire. Once out of sight, however, she paused. She had no idea what to look for. She took a few steps in one direction, stopped, retraced her steps, then moved off in another direction. Then she caught herself.

This is nonsense, she told herself. It is not like me to be so confused. Think, Catryn! Just *think* for a moment. She closed her eyes.

"If you truly need, and have the necessary faith, it will be delivered to you."

"We are in need," she said aloud. Then she opened her eyes. Not two paces away from her a small tree bloomed. White flowers covered its branches, but, at the same time, nestled amongst them, grew fruit. Green and lumpy, just as she had remembered. She hurried to fill the sack she had brought with her, then returned to Norl.

The boy had not budged. He stood exactly where she had left him, staring into the trees. When she emerged, a huge smile split his face.

"Here," she said. "Eat. You have never before tasted anything so wonderful."

When they had gorged themselves to their fullest, they pulled their cloaks around them and settled down for the night. Norl curled himself close to Catryn. In the cool darkness, the warmth of his small body was welcome. Only then, replete with the goodness of the deliverance fruit, did she allow herself to think of what had happened between them. How was it that he could hear her thoughts? Who was this child?

The next morning, as they trotted away from their camp—Catryn in her cat form, Norl now riding easily—Catryn suddenly paused. Something in the air attracted her senses. She pricked her ears. Her whiskers twitched. She threw up her muzzle and scented the air.

"What is it?" Norl asked, but she was too intent to answer.

There was something here. She could feel it.

Get off, Norl, she ordered.

"Why . . . ?" He stared around, instantly fearful.

There is nothing to fear, Catryn thought quickly. *But there is something . . . something here . . .*

Norl slid off her back and Catryn resumed her own form. She lost her cat sense, but could still feel a tingling running down her spine. There was magic here, she could sense it. She took a hesitant step forward and felt herself running up against a wall. An invisible wall.

"Catryn?" Norl's voice was taut.

"It's all right." She smiled. "Come here, Norl.

Stand beside me." She raised her hands and began to unfasten the air in front of them. Bit by bit, she worked a gap wide, from high above her head right down almost to the ground.

"Come." She took Norl's hand and led him through.

As she had suspected they would, they stepped out into more forest, but she knew where she was. She had found the portal Launan had used to spy on them that first day of their journey. They had reached Daunus.

Quickly, she changed back into cat form. *We will run as fast as possible to the city,* she told Norl. *Then I'll change back again and we will go to meet Dahl.*

Norl nodded. He looked a little dazed, but bursting with curiosity as well.

"How did you do that?" he asked. "Where are we now? What . . . ?"

We are close to Daunus, Catryn broke in, forestalling further queries. *Mount, Norl. There is no time for questions.*

She felt him clamber up on her back, then clasp her tightly. He laid his cheek against her neck. She could feel his warm breath, smell the good boy smell of him. Unconsciously, she began to purr—a deep, rumbling purr. "How do you do *that*?" Norl asked now. "I've always wondered how cats purr."

Be quiet, Norl. Hold on tightly, Catryn answered. She was not about to tell him that she didn't know herself.

They broke out of the trees and there, shimmering in the sunlight in the middle of the wide plain that lay before them, rose the walls of Daunus.

Catryn sent a quick mind scan into the city. All seemed normal. She raced across the plain and up to the gate, which was closed. A guard's face peered out from a narrow window. She could see the astonishment in his eyes. That was a good sign. At least his mind was there. The astonishment turned to fear as Norl jumped off her back and she shook herself back into her own form.

"Open the gates," she commanded. "Catryn, Seer of Taun, has business with your king."

The gates swung open immediately. Catryn swept past the dumbfounded guard, dragging Norl behind her. The boy was swiveling his head, trying to see everything at once and tripping over his feet at almost every step in the process.

"It's beautiful!" he cried. "I've never seen anything so grand!"

Relief flooded through Catryn. They had made it in time! The streets were thronged with people. People who sang and called out greetings to each other.

Then the relief ebbed and turned again to concern. These people—so happy and so innocent. They knew not the danger that was almost certainly bearing down upon them. She must get to Dahl's palace as quickly as possible.

CHAPTER 15

Was Dahl here already? Catryn wondered. The question was answered as she and Norl approached the palace gates, which opened to let out orderly squads of marching guards.

"Take cover," one called out to her as they passed by. "Return to your home and stay inside."

She watched as the lines of men flowed down into the city. They were disciplined and business-like. There was no panic. People questioned at first but, gradually, Catryn could see them beginning to desert the streets and take shelter in their houses. Good, she thought. As long as they stay indoors they will be safe. She cast an anxious glance at the shadows she and Norl were casting—long in the rising sunshine.

"Come, Norl," she said.

The guard at the palace gate would have turned them back, but Catryn had no time for him. Her eyes blazed as she fixed him with a fierce glare.

"I am Catryn, Seer of Taun," she declared. "Do you dare detain me?"

The guard melted back, motioning her through with a bow and jumbled words of apology.

Norl was impressed. "Are you *so* important, then?" he asked in a whisper.

"I am," Catryn replied.

"And you are going to save all these people?" he asked further. "They will not have their souls stolen from them as did the people in my village? As did my mother?" His voice broke on the last words.

"I am," Catryn answered again without hesitation, her voice as determined and firm as she could make it.

But how was she going to do it? In truth, she was nowhere near as confident as she made herself sound. Then she pushed that question out of her mind. First of all, she must find Dahl. And was Sele the Plump here, too? Just what did the Sele have planned?

She marched up to the massive front door and through it. Guards scattered as she strode in. Holding tightly onto Norl, she made her way to Dahl's private rooms. There was an air of uneasy bustle throughout the palace, but no sign of panic. When she reached

Dahl's chamber she pulled back the heavy curtain in the doorway and went in. Dahl was seated at a low table, talking to Coraun. Deep frown lines—almost lines of despair, it seemed—lined the older man's face.

"Again?" he was saying as Catryn entered. "Are we really to face enslavement again?"

"No," Dahl answered, "I will not allow it. Then he leaped to his feet as he saw her. "Catryn!" he exclaimed. "You are well come indeed! How did you get here so quickly?"

"Is the Sele here?" she asked instead. Explanations could follow later.

Dahl's forehead creased into frown lines as well, then smoothed. "No," he said. "I have seen no sign of it. But we are taking precautions and we will be ready for the beast when she comes." His hand strayed to the pommel of his sword.

Brave words, Catryn thought, but she was dismayed nonetheless. She had not realized how much she had been counting on Sele the Plump.

"The people are receiving orders to stay indoors," Dahl went on. "If they do not go out, the beast will not be able to snatch their shadows away."

"A temporary measure only," Catryn said. "They will not be able to stay inside indefinitely. What if she just waits?"

"Then I will kill her," Dahl said. His face was pale, the dragon scar throbbed scarlet, but his voice was firm. "I shall kill her or she will kill me. One or the other."

Catryn's heart stopped for a moment. "*We* will kill her," she said. "We will do battle together."

"As we did before," Dahl said.

"Yes," Catryn agreed. "As we did before."

Dahl reached out to take her hand. The warmth of his grasp was familiar and comforting. "We must make plans," he said. "Come, sit with us. You have met Coraun, I believe?"

The three of them bent to their work. Forgotten, Norl stood watching them.

"I will shield you as best I can, Dahl," Catryn said. "When the dragon attacks and is concentrating entirely on you, she will be at her weakest. I am certain I can shield you from her fire."

"And I will fly up under her and strike at the vulnerable spot on the underside of her neck, as I did with her child. I killed him that way; I shall slay her in the same manner."

That reminded Catryn of Norl. She looked around for him and saw him standing, his mouth slightly agape.

"You must stay here, Norl," she said. "In this room. In here you will be safe. Do you understand?"

The boy nodded.

"I mean what I say," Catryn repeated. "You must not go outside."

"I won't," Norl answered. His face was even whiter than Dahl's, but he stood firm.

What is it about this boy? Catryn thought. He is definitely not like any other boy I have ever known.

"My mother said I was special," Norl said.

Was he reading her thoughts again?

"She said that was why she feared so for me," he said.

"All children are special to their parents," Catryn answered, but even as she spoke the words, she knew there was something more here. And, it would seem, Mavahn knew it as well.

"Catryn?"

Dahl's voice brought her out of her wonderings.

"We are going to patrol the town. Make certain everyone is inside. You will come?"

"Of course," Catryn replied. "The maidservant will bring you food," she said to Norl. "Remember your promise—you will stay here?"

"I will," Norl said.

By the time they left the palace, the streets were deserted except for the guards.

"What of them?" Catryn asked. "They will be in danger."

"They have orders to take cover as soon as the beast appears," Dahl answered. "You and I will fight her alone."

Catryn nodded, but she could not keep from casting her eyes across the plain into the woods beyond.

Where was the Sele? What had happened to it?

When they had satisfied themselves that all the townspeople had taken shelter, Dahl turned to Coraun. "You must return to the palace," he said. "It is necessary that you be in a place of safety. In case . . ." He did not continue.

Coraun looked as if he would argue, then nodded his head. "I will do as you command, my king," he said. "But I like it not."

Dahl clasped the man's hand in both of his own. "You must stay safe," he repeated. "Daunus needs you."

Coraun grasped Dahl's hands tightly, then turned back toward the palace.

Catryn swiveled to look all around her.

"It is so quiet," she said. "So strange!"

"The people remember what things were like before," Dahl answered. "They know enough to hide now."

"Where is the horse?" Catryn asked then.

"In the shelter of the main gate. I left it hidden there. It is time, now, I think, for us to return to it."

"Good," Catryn replied.

They made their way to the archway of the gate. Catryn glanced repeatedly at the sky, ready to break into a run if any shadow appeared on the horizon. None did, however, and they reached its shelter safely. A guard stood underneath the stone arch. It was the same guard who had admitted Catryn earlier. He bowed to Dahl and looked at Catryn in fear.

The horse greeted them with soft snufflings and pawed at the cobblestones with one hoof. Its eyes glowed, the fire within them banked, but growing. As Dahl took the blanket off its back, it shook out its wings and unfurled them, spreading them out to their full magnificence. Dahl mounted, unsheathed his sword and held it ready. Catryn stood beside him.

They waited.

The sun rose to its zenith and began its descent. The afternoon shadows lengthened. Still they waited.

"No!"

Catryn heard Dahl's quick intake of breath. She followed his worried stare to see a few people peering tentatively out of their houses. Even as she watched, one young woman stepped out of her doorway, cast a quick glance at the sky and then scampered down the path to the well. Another, seeing her, ran after her. Then a man nipped out of a back door and began to gather vegetables. One by one, more people emerged from their houses until the streets were once again thronged with people.

"What are they doing?" Dahl exclaimed incredulously.

It was the hour of the evening meal, Catryn realized. The people were hungry, and they must have thought it was safe since all looked so peaceful.

"They must return!" Dahl cried. He kicked hard into the horse's sides and sent the animal into a startled gallop. "Guards!" Dahl shouted, "make those people take cover!"

"Dahl! Come back!" Catryn cried, but he did not hear. At the sound of his horse's hooves, those who had emerged from their houses began to run back, but it was too late.

A shadow blotted out the sun. For an instant all was thrown into a dim penumbra, then the sun broke free again and the stink of dragon filled the air.

The beast swept down upon them, its wings making a sound as loud as thunder. People screamed. The guards, taken by surprise, turned to face the dragon, swords drawn. Dahl reined in the horse, leaned over its neck to speak a few words that Catryn could not hear, then the horse leaped into the air.

Catryn sent out a shielding with every bit of strength she possessed. But she could shield only Dahl—the guards and the people in the streets were exposed. She could not protect them.

And then, as if they had appeared by magic itself, the streets were suddenly filled with throngs of the Sele.

"Stay where you are!" they cried with one voice. The command rang loudly through the streets. The people and the guards alike froze in astonishment. Even the dragon seemed to hover motionless. One Sele ran to each person. And sat. On their shadow. In an instant, every shadow of every living being was covered by a Sele.

The dragon emitted a shriek of fury. She circled the town, swooping low, then rose back sunward. She turned upon Dahl. Catryn, as astonished as the rest, had let her shield weaken. Just in time, she intensified it again. The dragon screamed with rage and turned toward her. A sheet of flame spewed forth from her throat. Catryn braced herself. She felt the flame sear into the space around her. She felt herself begin to weaken. Then, just as she knew she could hold on no longer, the dragon swerved in the air again. Dahl and the horse were coming straight up at her from below. Dahl held his sword high. The horse veered to the side at the last possible moment, and Dahl struck. But the dragon had seen him in time. She, too, veered away, and he missed.

The dragon made one last flight over the city. People cowered in fear, but none ran. It seemed as if they were anchored in place by the protecting Sele.

Catryn shifted her mind shield, trying to protect the exposed people and the Sele, but she could not extend it so far. Surely the dragon would unleash her fire upon them! But, to Catryn's astonishment, after her last swoop across the city the beast rose again. She banked and flew directly at Catryn.

The battle is yours. This time.

The words seared into Catryn's brain.

But I will be back!

And then she disappeared into the northern sky.

The silence after she left was profound, but the air hung heavy with the smell of fire. One by one, the Sele got up and melted back into the gathering shadows of the city walls.

"Wait," Catryn cried, but they vanished as quickly

as they had appeared. All except Sele the Plump. Dahl landed beside her. The horse was breathing in great gulps of air. There was a smell of singed hair about it, but it was unhurt. Dahl's face was taut with a fury equal to the dragon's.

"Twice!" he cried. "Twice I have failed!"

"She is more knowledgeable than her child," Sele the Plump said. "More devious. She will be much harder to vanquish."

"How did you do that?" Catryn asked. "You and the other Sele? How did you save the townsfolk? Why did the dragon not send her flames down to demolish you? I had no shielding over you. I could not."

"The dragons cannot harm us," the Sele answered. "Nor can we harm them. It was a blood pact made between our two species back at the beginning of this world, so we have been told. Sele the Parent, the first of our kind, mingled his blood with the blood of the parent dragon of them all and they swore an unbreakable vow that we would live together in peace."

"Why?" Dahl asked. "Why would you make such a pact?"

"Why not?" the Sele asked mildly. "We posed no threat to the dragons. They were peaceful then—it is your people who stirred them up to war—but we were mindful of the fact that they could do us much harm, if for some reason they wished to do so. It behooved us to ensure our well-being. Perhaps if you humans could stop making war on each other, stop making use of the beasts to kill each other, you might be able to forge such a pact yourselves."

Dahl stared at the Sele for a long moment. The fury drained from his face.

"You speak the truth," he said finally. "And if it were up to me, I would dearly love to do so. I would dearly love to live in peace. But, unfortunately, it is not up to me."

"Not now," the Sele said. "Perhaps, sometime . . . ?" He shrugged. "We never know what you humans will do," it said. "The dragons are more predictable at least."

They made their way back to the palace.

"Now, Catryn, we will do as you wished. We will track the beast down to her lair," Dahl said as they entered his chamber again. "Despite your talk of peace," he said to Sele the Plump, "she must be slain. Perhaps sometime in the future we will be able to live at peace with these beasts, but for now we cannot. She may be constrained by her blood pact with you, but she has sided with the forces that are trying to destroy *my* world and I *must* kill her." He drew his sword and began honing it with a stone. His movements were sharp and angry again. "Will your people stay here to protect the townsfolk while we are gone?"

"We will," Sele the Plump answered. "As long as we are needed. We would like to see an end to all of this as much as you would."

"You said once that it had not been given to your people to know for what purpose you were created," Catryn said slowly. "Perhaps it might be for this? To help us find a way to end the strife?"

"Perhaps," the Sele answered. It looked around, as if suddenly remembering something. "Where is the boy, Norl?" it asked.

"He is here," Catryn said. She looked around as well but, to her dismay, she did not see him. She felt suddenly cold.

"Norl?" she called. She pulled the covers of Dahl's bed back, hoping to find him nestled down amongst them, asleep. He was not there. The cold turned to ice as she darted out of the room. A maidservant was just approaching.

"Where is the boy?" Catryn demanded, her voice so harsh that the maid gaped at her in astonishment. "The boy, Norl, whom I left here. Where is he?"

"Why, he went with the messenger you sent for him," the girl answered. "The man in the cloak. He was very nice, that man was. Did he not take the boy to you? He said he was going to."

Launan! He had stolen Norl away!

CHAPTER 16

Catryn rushed back into Dahl's chamber. "Launan has taken Norl!" She reached out a hand to Dahl.

"Launan was here?" Dahl asked, stunned.

"Yes. While we were fighting the dragon. He came here and took Norl!"

"Why would he do that?" Dahl asked. "Why is that boy of such importance to Launan that he would risk coming here to steal him away from us?" Then, as he took her hand, he exclaimed. "You're as cold as ice, Catryn. And shaking! Why is the boy of such importance to *you*? I would understand concern, but this is beyond concern."

With an effort, Catryn brought herself under control.

"I know not why that boy is so important, Dahl," she said, steadying her voice as much as she could. "But he is. There is something special about him.

"And I think I know why Launan took him," she rushed on. "He is going to give him to the dragon. She wants him."

"The dragon wants Norl? Why?" Dahl asked incredulously.

"Revenge, perhaps. But I think even more than that. Norl is in mortal danger, Dahl. We must rescue him!"

Dahl reached for his sword and strapped it on.

"Launan cannot be far ahead of us," he said grimly. "We will reach the dragon's lair as soon as he does." He turned to Sele the Plump. "Will you stay here to ensure the safety of the city?" he asked.

"I will," the Sele replied.

Dahl mounted the winged horse, then helped Catryn up behind him. The horse took their weight easily. With two strong wingbeats it was aloft and heading toward the cliff where the dragon dwelt. Catryn held tightly onto Dahl. Her mind was in a torrent of confusion but then, mingled with the howling of the wind that tore at Dahl's cloak and clawed at her tangled, wild-blowing hair, came a singing. Catryn closed her eyes. She welcomed the aura of the Elders into her mind, shutting out all else. But it was not a reassuring song this time. There was foreboding in it. Concern.

The child must be saved, Catryn, the music inside her mind said. *He must not be given over to them.*

"Catryn!" Dahl's voice broke the enchantment. He turned his head toward her and shouted into the wind. "Look there!" He pointed to the earth below.

She came back to herself with a jolt and looked down. The singing ceased as if cut off.

The mountainside under them was split into a deep fissure. Catryn shuddered as she recognized the ledge on which she had lain after falling over the edge. From here it looked like such a small outcropping and the drop down into the depths below was so great.

Dahl guided the horse in tighter and tighter circles. Into the cleft, below the ledge, finally down to the very bottom. It was so narrow here and choked with trees that landing was difficult. As soon as the horse had set its hooves upon the earth, Dahl jumped off and reached up to help Catryn.

"I will lead the horse now," he said. "It will be easier to search for the opening to the dragon's cave on foot. It must be close by." He rested his hand on the hilt of his sword.

"I will search in my own way," Catryn said. "Follow me." She shifted back into her lioness body. She cast her nose up and savored the air. The scent of trees and dark earth filled her nostrils. Her whiskers twitched. She cocked first one ear and then the other.

One scent came to her over all others. A thickly dark and evil stink. She knew it came from the dragon's lair. Casting a quick glance behind her to ensure that Dahl was following, she began to pad lightly along an almost imperceptible path that led through the underbrush, toward the cliffside. She wove her way skillfully through the matted bushes, breaking a trail for Dahl and the horse. She wished she could speak with him—soon she would have to return to her human form, but not yet. She made her way through one particularly thick patch, then broke through into a kind of opening. The smell of fire and singed vegetation and something more obscene assaulted her nostrils. She halted. Dahl broke through behind her, then came to a stop as well. In front of them yawned an opening in the cliff, almost as high as the cliff itself. It looked as if it had been blasted out by a lightning stroke of unbelievable power. Inside the opening—blackness. Blackness such as Catryn had never seen. Blackness so black it seemed solid.

It was time. Catryn shifted back.

"Wait, Dahl," she said as Dahl unsheathed his sword. She laid a restraining hand on his arm and cast her mind ahead of them.

Chaos!

She was met with a miasma of emotions. Anger and fury, rimmed with fire—the dragon knew they were coming! But beyond that, underneath it somehow and yet all around it, waves of desolation. Of bereavement. For a moment Catryn was at a loss to understand it, and then the realization came to her: it was the despair of the stolen souls she was sensing. So they were there!

"The dragon knows we are coming, Dahl," she said then. "She has the souls of all the people there in her keeping, and she will do whatever she can to keep us from them."

Dahl did not answer. Catryn looked at him, taken aback by what she saw. His eyes were dark with fury; the dragon scar on his cheek burned. He looked around, searching, then broke off a branch from a tree. With tinder and flint, he set about trying to make a flame.

It was too slow! Feverish with impatience, Catryn sent a spell spinning into the branch. The end of it broke into flame. Dahl drew back, startled, but recovered himself quickly. He picked the torch up, held it aloft and strode into the cave.

Catryn hesitated for a moment. He had not given thought to the horse. Should they leave it to wait for them here? That would, perhaps, be the most sensible thing to do.

No. They would need it; somehow, she knew that.

"Follow," she commanded and the horse obeyed.

The light from the torch wavered and seemed swallowed up by the density of the darkness that lay before them. Nevertheless, Dahl strode into it. The opening was large, but it soon tapered down into a narrow passageway, barely wide enough for them. Catryn cast her mind ahead of them, shielding them as they made their way. Dahl marched on without hesitation, but she felt herself growing weaker and weaker. The maelstrom awaiting them assaulted her mind and battered her unceasingly. The effort of shielding became harder and harder. She stumbled, but did not allow herself to fall. She had to keep pace with Dahl. She could not let him face the dragon alone.

Dahl stopped so suddenly that she, lost in her concentration, almost bumped into him. He drew his breath in with a gasp. Catryn moved to stand beside him, then she, too, caught her breath at what lay before them.

A pit gaped at their feet, huge in its expanse. Rising up from it came wisps of smoke. Fire flickered in the depths, casting light enough that their pitiful torch was no longer needed. More light streamed down from above. Catryn looked up. Far above them, an opening revealed a glimpse of the sky. She looked down again.

The dragon lay coiled at the bottom of the abyss. She stared at them, eyes huge and blazing. She seemed to be lying on a cushion of darkness. A cushion that shifted and writhed as if in pain. Catryn reeled back with the force of the turmoil that rose up to greet her. Even as she gathered herself to withstand the impact, however, her mind was working.

"If we can induce her to leave her nest," she said, "I can try to set those souls free."

"I will challenge her," Dahl said. "She cannot refuse me."

"But if I am concentrating on releasing the souls, I will not be able to shield you," Catryn protested.

"Then I will fight unshielded. It is good that you brought the horse. He and I will fight together again."

"Her power is much greater than her child's . . ." Catryn began, then stopped, her words cut off in horror.

Three figures appeared out of an opening on the edge of the pit just beyond them—two tall, one small. Launan and Bruhn! And between them, held securely by Launan, was Norl.

"Caulda!" Launan called out. The word echoed and reechoed throughout the chamber.

The dragon breathed out a great rush of fire. "Who dares to name me?" she roared, aloud this time, and cast her head from side to side.

"I, Launan, your master, call you. I have that right. And the power."

"You have." The words hissed after the retreating echoes of her name. Caulda focused her gaze now on Launan.

"And I am your master—acknowledge it!" Launan seemed to grow taller, more menacing, as he stared back at the beast.

Catryn held her breath as Caulda's voice burned through the space between them.

"You are."

"I have brought you that which you desired, Caulda," Launan called. "The child. He is yours. And in return . . ."

"In return?" The question slithered through the air and hung there.

"In return, you will destroy the King of Taun and his Seer."

"I will do as you command," Caulda replied. "It will be a small matter. I have but toyed with them before."

"Not so small as you might wish, Caulda!" Dahl cried. "I challenge you, dragon beast!"

Caulda swung her head around at the sound of Dahl's voice. Launan and Bruhn looked over, as well. Catryn thought she saw Bruhn flinch at the sight of them.

"First the child," Caulda replied, looking back to Launan. "Throw him down to me."

"No!" Catryn screamed, but Launan had already caught up the boy. He raised him high, ready to cast him into the abyss.

Catryn was astride the horse in one bound. The animal needed no orders—he surged into the air toward Launan, just as Launan threw Norl down.

The horse swerved, folded his wings and plummeted earthward. Catryn stretched out. Norl was falling toward her—just out of reach. The horse swerved yet again, and Catryn reached with her mind as well as her arms. Norl fell into them with a jolt that nearly unseated her. At the same moment, a blast of fire shot up from below. Catryn shielded them just in time. Even so, the fire singed and burned.

The dragon shrieked. With a noise as of thunder, she unfurled her wings and rose toward Catryn, leaving her nest unguarded. Now! Catryn dropped the shielding and concentrated instead on the moving darkness below her.

Take your freedom! she commanded. *Escape!*

Slowly, then more and more quickly, the darkness began to rise. It shredded and separated into shards. Each shard gathered speed, then sped upward, toward the opening so far above. There was no time to watch, however; the dragon was almost upon her. Again, Catryn threw her mind out toward the beast.

"Back! Away!" she cried to the horse and it whirled, climbing and circling to escape the beast.

"I challenge you! Do you fear me, Caulda?" Dahl's voice rang out again. The dragon paused, hovered in the air. Dahl stood poised on the brink of the abyss, sword drawn.

Catryn felt her heart seize with terror. She had left him unprotected! In that very instant she saw Launan appear behind him.

"Dahl!" she screamed the warning, but it was too

late. Launan stretched out both hands. Light streamed from his fingertips. It flashed out toward Dahl but, before it could reach him, a form threw itself in between. Bruhn! Dahl whipped around in time to see the full force of the light strike Bruhn instead of him. Bruhn's body lifted into the air as if thrown by an invisible giant's hand. He hung suspended for a moment, then plummeted into the depths.

A cry of anguish issued forth from Dahl's throat. He raised his sword high and struck. Launan, taken by surprise, reeled with the force of the blow and staggered. He took a step backward—into space. One great, despairing scream arose from him as he fell, twisting and turning. Then there was silence.

Catryn stared. Two bodies sprawled on the ground far beneath. Neither moved. Then she came to herself. The dragon!

"Back to Dahl," she cried to the horse. They dove down to land beside him and, dragging Norl behind her, she leaped off its back to face Caulda.

A sheet of flame raced out to meet her. Catryn countered it, but weakly. Her power was almost exhausted. The dragon seemed to sense it.

You cannot hold out against me. Words meant this time for Catryn alone.

Give me the boy and you can both go.

You would give up Dahl's kingdom? Catryn shot back.

I care not for kingdoms, came the answer. *I but obeyed a power greater than my own and that is gone now. I will give you your lives. But I must have the boy. You stole my treasure—I will have the boy in exchange. And I will have my revenge.*

The words of the Elders reverberated in Catryn's mind. She must not give him up. *No,* she answered. *You will not have him.*

"What is happening, Catryn?"

Dahl's question jolted her into an awareness of him. She looked at him and could not recognize him. His face was drawn tightly over the skull beneath. His eyes flamed and the dragon scar on his cheek burned blood red.

"She wants Norl," Catryn replied. "I will not give him to her."

"Never," Dahl said, the single word filled with hate. He turned to face the dragon again, sword at the ready.

"Are you so afraid of me that you will not take up my challenge?" he cried.

Paugh! Does this puny human truly believe he can defeat me? The dragon's wings beat more rapidly. She hovered closer.

"He defeated your child," Catryn shot back, aloud. She could feel Dahl's hatred invading her, taking her over as well. Together they could destroy this beast. They *would* destroy her!

Caulda spread her wings. Her mouth gaped wide, and curved, needle-pointed teeth glistened as a tongue of flame whipped out to scorch the ground at their feet.

"Yessss! So he did!" Her voice hissed out, filling the cavern with its sound.

"I did!" Dahl cried, "and I will slay you as well!"

Catryn gathered every fragment of power remaining to her and prepared to hurl it at the dragon.

"Wait!" The cry rang out. "Spare them! I will come back to you if you spare them!"

Catryn whipped around to see Norl standing on the very edge of the precipice, almost leaning into Caulda's fire.

"What are you saying, Norl?" she cried. "What are you doing?" She reached for him, but he eluded her grasp.

"Get out of the way, Norl!" Dahl shouted. He grabbed Norl and thrust the boy behind him, then braced himself against the fury of the dragon.

Desperately, Catryn reached to regain her power. She must shield them!

Caulda checked her attack.

"You would return of your own volition?" The words blew hotly over them.

"I will. When the time is right."

"Norl!" Again Catryn reached for him but again he eluded her. He slid out from behind Dahl to face Caulda.

"I give you my word," he said. He stood rock still and stared straight into the fiery depths of the dragon's eyes.

Slowly, the fire dimmed in those great eyes. Slowly, she hooded them.

"So," she replied, "this is how it is meant to be?"

"It is," Norl said.

"No!" Catryn cried. "You cannot do this, Norl!"

"I can," Norl replied. He seemed strangely calm. "I must."

"I cannot let you," Catryn cried again. "I *will* not let you, Norl. You know not what you do."

"But I do! I know it with every fiber of my being. Trust me, Catryn. This is the way."

Trust! Again! But how could she? Surely this child could not be allowed to make such a promise?

Let me do this, Catryn.

Norl's thought came clearly through to her. And just as clearly came the knowledge that in this she, Catryn, Seer of Taun, must give way. She *must* trust. This was not for her to decide.

With an effort greater than any effort she had ever made in her life, Catryn turned from Norl and faced Caulda.

"The decision is his to make," she said.

Dahl reached out yet again for Norl, but Catryn stayed his hands.

Caulda hung in the air, slit-eyed.

"Will you accept my pledge?" Norl called.

"Yesss," she hissed finally. "I will." She swung her massive head up high and stared now, wide-eyed, at the three figures standing before her. Flame surged briefly from her throat but stopped short of them. "Go, then, all of you," she commanded. She lowered her head until her eyes were on a level with Norl.

They flared briefly. He did not flinch.

I will await you, boy. When it is time. She did not speak the words aloud. They were meant for Norl alone. Norl and Catryn.

The dragon gave two thunderous flaps of her wings, then rose up and disappeared into the blueness of the sky beyond.

Catryn turned to Dahl. He stood, sword dangling from his hand, staring after the dragon. As she watched, the fire left his eyes as well. The dragon scar flared once, then began to fade. The flesh seemed to return to his bones.

"So we have won," he said.

"We have," Catryn answered.

"And Taun is safe."

"It is."

"I cannot believe it is over." He rubbed his eyes with one hand.

"But it is," Catryn said. "For us." She reached to put an arm around Norl.

Then Dahl lowered his gaze and stared down at the broken bodies below.

"My friend," he whispered. His eyes were bright again, but with tears, not anger this time.

Only then did Catryn notice the horse. The drag-onfire had not spared him. He stood, trembling, head low. His forelegs were burned black and blistered.

Catryn gave a cry. She would have gone to him, but Norl was there first. The boy put out his hands, caressed the horse's legs tenderly. As she watched, the skin healed, the gray hair grew back. The horse raised his head. He snuffled softly and pushed his broad forehead into Norl's hands.

"How . . . ?" Catryn began.

Norl looked up at her. His eyes were wide with wonder.

"He was in pain," he said.

CHAPTER 17

Despite their victory, the journey back to the cave of the Elders was a somber one. Dahl spoke not at all. Deep lines etched his face; he seemed to have aged by years. He rode the horse, while Catryn padded beside him in lioness form. Only Norl was ebullient and happy, a young boy once more, seemingly forgetful of all that had happened. He rode on Catryn's back with familiar ease. But, upon reaching the cave, the appearance of the Elders themselves and the Protector subdued him.

"You have done well, Dahl and Catryn," Ygrauld

said. As usual, they were seated in the brilliant cavern.

As Catryn was about to answer, she was surprised to see Sele the Plump appear out of one of the openings.

"You left Daunus?" Dahl asked. They were the first words he had spoken since leaving the dragon's lair.

"We sent for the Sele," Ronauld said. "As soon as it was known that the people of Daunus were no longer in danger and it was not needed there. The Sele have done their part to save Taun, as well. They must be acknowledged."

"That they must," Dahl agreed. "We have much to thank you for, friend Sele."

"And you, Dahl, you have done well," the Sele said. "Launan is dead and Taun is safe once more." It paused. "But the force that gave him power exists still. We must not forget that."

There was silence for a moment, then Ygrauld spoke.

"As there is goodness in the world, so must there be evil. It is a never-ending battle."

The Sele nodded. "It is so," it said. Then it turned once more to Dahl. "I sorrow with you over the death of your friend."

"He betrayed me," Dahl said.

"He did," Catryn broke in. "Nothing can change that. But in the end he gave his life for you, Dahl."

"Catryn speaks the truth." Tauna rose. "Whatever

Bruhn did, he redeemed himself. He saved you, Dahl, and he saved Taun."

"And now," Catryn said, "I have a question."

"I thought you might," the Elder woman replied.

"This boy, Norl, who is he?" Catryn pulled him forward. He blushed, but drew himself up to stand as tall as he could beside her. "He is no ordinary boy, that I have discovered."

"No, he is not," the woman answered. She came forward, leaned down and took both of Norl's hands in her own. "Look at me, Norl," she commanded.

Norl did as he was bade.

"From time to time we scour your old world, Catryn, seeking for babes such as yourself and this boy. Babes who are born with gifts your world would deny—would persecute you for. We did not find you but, fortunately, you found us. Norl, however, we did find. Abandoned, unloved and feared from the moment of his birth. The folk who raised him knew not what made him different, but they sensed enough to be afraid of him. We rescued him from an early death and brought him here. He was given to Mavahn to care for until he became old enough to learn what he will need to learn."

"Mavahn is not my mother?" Norl's voice came out in a gasp.

"She *is* your mother. In every way that is important, Norl, Mavahn is your mother. She has cared for you and loved you since we gave you to her. She has never thought of you as anything but her own."

"Then it was no accident that we found him," Catryn said.

"No, it was not an accident."

Catryn paused. "He ... he made a vow. To the dragon. To Caulda ..." She felt Norl stiffen beside her.

"To return to her?"

"Yes."

"I thought as much," Tauna said. "I know Caulda from of old."

"But what should he do?" Catryn asked. "What will happen to him?"

"That is his fate, Catryn. Did I not tell you, you must have trust?"

"You did," Catryn answered slowly.

"You will do your part, never fear," Tauna said.

"You will take him home to Mavahn, Catryn." It was the Protector who spoke now, his voice stronger than it had been. "He will stay with her until his thirteenth birthday. At that time you will fetch him and bring him back to us. Then it will be you, Catryn, who will be the teacher, and he will be your pupil."

Norl cast a quick look at Catryn. "Will you show me how to become a cat?" he asked, eyes shining now. "Will you teach me how to purr?"

Catryn laughed. "I doubt you will be a cat, my little one. A bird, I should think. A bright, high-flying bird." She looked at the Protector as she spoke the words and he returned the smile that lightened her face.

"Yes," he said. "I should think so."

"And I will fly?"

"You will fly," the Protector answered.

Catryn and Dahl sat alone and silent in his chambers. Norl had been taken back to his mother; Sele the Plump had returned to his people. Dahl sprawled beside the fire, his face almost hidden in the flickering shadows cast by the flames. It was Catryn's turn now to wait until Dahl was ready to speak. Finally, he leaned forward to stir up the embers, then turned to look at her. His eyes were dark, but calm. The Usurper slept.

"So you return to the Elders now?" He said. It was not really a question.

"Yes," Catryn answered. "There is much still to learn. And then I must teach Norl. You heard the Protector's words. This is my duty."

"And it is my duty to stay here and govern my people," Dahl replied. "To care for them." He nodded, with acceptance of the charge. He stared at her as if memorizing the curves and hollows of her face.

Catryn waited. Their quest was over. The time for decisions had come.

"You are even more beautiful than when you left,

Catryn," Dahl said then. "And just as young. You will stay this way forever, will you not?"

So—he had been thinking on her immortality, too.

"I will age. You've seen the Elders . . ."

"But not in my lifetime. Will you age during my lifetime, Catryn?"

"No." The barest of whispers.

Dahl fell silent again. He sank back into the shadows and stared into the fire. Catryn knew before he did what his next question would be.

"I could live with that. Could you?"

"Here? In Daunus?"

"Yes. Later. When you have fulfilled your obligation to Norl."

Catryn held herself still. She closed her eyes. Unbidden, the scents and secrets of the world that were only open to her in her animal form flooded her mind. Even now, even as she sat here, they called to her. She chafed at the walls surrounding her. The comfort of the pillows on which she reclined grated. She began to speak. Slowly. Choosing her words with care.

"You have made Daunus beautiful, Dahl," she said. "But no matter how much love I bear you, and it is much, I could never live here. This is not the way for me."

"I feared so," he said. "But you will return? From time to time—when you can?"

"I will," Catryn promised.

Early the next morning, with the dawn of the sun, Catryn slipped out of the palace. The dew was heavy on the grass as she hastened through the city gates. Only when she was out of sight of the guards, out of sight of Daunus itself, did she pause. A shimmer, a slight rearranging of space, then a lithe young wildcat that glowed golden in the early morning sunlight stretched and shook off the constraints of her human form. Catryn raised her muzzle to the currents of the air. She drew them in deeply, savoring every secret nuance. Then she began to run. Smoothly, effortlessly, into the deep shadows of the welcoming forest.

Home.